GUN CHANCE

Center Point
Large Print

Also by Giff Cheshire and available from
Center Point Large Print:

Thunder on the Mountain
Renegade River
Night Riders

GUN CHANCE

GIFF CHESHIRE

CENTER POINT LARGE PRINT
THORNDIKE, MAINE

This Center Point Large Print edition
is published in the year 2025 by arrangement with
Golden West Inc.

Copyright © 1957 by Graphic Publishing Company, Inc.

All rights reserved.

The text of this Large Print edition is unabridged.
In other aspects, this book may vary
from the original edition.
Printed in the United States of America
on permanent paper sourced using
environmentally responsible foresting methods.
Set in 16-point Times New Roman type.

ISBN: 979-8-89164-607-0

The Library of Congress has cataloged this record
under Library of Congress Control Number: 2025934461

1

The rimrock where Nick Marquis lay hidden was almost too hot to touch. He didn't feel it. Instead a harsh anger made its pulsing way through him as he stared at the activity beyond. The sheep camp was breaking up, getting ready to cross the deadline into cattle country, breaching all agreements.

Sounds reached him vaguely through the heat haze.

"Alfonso, hurry them saddle horses!" somebody yelled in the hidden distance. It sounded like Tripp Coyle, the grass pirate, hazing one of his Basque herders.

In sight by the rope corral the dusky camp tender was harnessing a team of mules, hurried and nervous looking. Over at the wagon the dark-skinned *cocinero* kept throwing stuff into a heap for loading. Two *anglos* stood watching, gunhawks whose rank made them despise such work. They had filed fresh notches on their six-guns since the tramp sheep outfit came out of California. They had small interest in lesser chores.

Slipping back from the rim, Nick came to his feet. For a moment his vision wavered from heat and the weight of hot blood on his brain.

He wiped a restless hand across his mouth and started walking in the brutal glare of the sun. He moved like a man driven by blind anger.

The formation he had climbed was a tilted *cuesta*, and he had left his horse in a boulder field on its lower edge. As he came in around the heated rocks an animal's formless sense of danger penetrated his emotion. He felt his neck muscles tighten, his nostrils swelling. A few steps later he could see his horse and two other objects, a tense, fiercely watching dog and a woman.

She held the bridle reins, and her features and the alert hostility of the dog told him he would have trouble getting hold of the horse. He thought of pulling his gun, but some ancient chivalry destroyed the impulse. That was another thing about the damned sheepers, he thought. They brought their women into their wars.

"You are the veree bad spy," the woman said in an odd, throaty accent, "and veree stupid, *vaquero*."

"You knew I was up there?" Nick asked in surprise. He had crawled in like a Piute for his look.

Carlita Corta—he had heard her name in Lilyville where men spoke bawdily of the beautiful girl traveling with the sheepmen—made a low, musical laugh. He saw strong white teeth behind lips red and full and contrasting vividly with her dark skin and hair. She glanced in pride and fondness at the sheep dog.

"Keeng, he know as soon as you get here. He tell me. He has reason to hate an *anglo* cowman, *vaquero*, as have I and my brothers."

"He going to let me have my horse?" Nick asked grimly.

"Only if I tell him I wish it so."

All the pent-up rage of the animal kingdom for those they hate in the world of men simmered in the yellow eyes of the sheep dog. The girl's mocking ones dared Nick to come closer, but he was too wise for that. And worried. She was playing with him, but her purpose was clear and deadly. If the sheepmen were really moving, a dead deadline rider would make one less gun to be contended with—a new warning to the other cowmen that Tripp Coyle could not be stopped.

"Then tell him you wish it so!" Nick said hotly.

"You are afraid of him?" Again that short, tuneful laugh.

Nick's answer punched out at her. "I know about Coyle and the ruin he's left behind him. Men who've died between here and the Black Rock trying to save their grass from his sheep. I see he's going to cross another deadline—into my country, this time."

The dark eyes twinkled. "How do you know he is not running away from the fight you threatened him with? Maybe he is going back where he came from."

Nick scowled. "You think it's funny to leave

ruined range and dead men behind your blasted sheep."

A queer fight came into the eyes of the girl at that. She shook her head. "There is very little, any more, that I think is funny. *Pastores* tied to the wheels of burning sheep wagons, women stripped naked and sheep clubbed to death— those things are not funny."

"Pull that dog away. I'm coming for my horse."

"No. We are going to see Tripp Coyle about this little matter of spying on our camp. You will walk ahead of me. If I let him, King will tear open your throat."

As he pulled his gun, the dog's bunched muscles burst into action. The girl forgot her mixed English and Spanish and cried out in the ancient tongue of her people. The pistol cracked loud and sharp in this confusion, the drive of the bullet turning the charging dog over in mid-air.

By then Nick had grasped the bridle reins and jerked them from the girl's hand. Her stricken, loathing eyes burned him, then swept to the dog.

"You'd rather have him rip my throat for me?" Nick grunted.

As she ran to the dropped animal, blind and deaf to him, Nick Marquis hit the saddle and whipped out. He knew the report of the shot had carried to the Coyle camp, where men had been saddling horses. He drove in the steel.

A Bosco loves his dog, he was thinking, and

it's like I shot some kid. He felt regret, even though she had forced him to do it. On the lower Owyhee and Humboldt there were many of her people now, self-isolated mostly, still as thoroughly Basque as they had even been on the sun-slopes of the Pyrenees. They were by nature a gay people, loving music and dancing, among themselves speaking a language few others could master and elsewhere using the mixed idiom they learned from the *anglos* and Mexicans. They loved sheep, were excellent herders, and for this reason and their proud personal courage they were in demand by roving sheepmen of Coyle's stripe. For that reason they had become thoroughly hated and some of them were no longer gay but bitter and dedicated, as was this Carlita Corta.

Safely over the land crest, Nick riveted his thoughts on more immediate problems. Here on the plateau, which lifted the Nevada-Idaho border a mile above sea level, the land offered little but rock and sandy earth, stunted sage and bunchgrass. But as it sloped down toward the Snake, on the Idaho side, it grew prolific in forage and became the seat of a thriving cattle industry. Boulder Basin, still ahead of him, lay between the headwaters of Salmon and Goose Creeks, and was its summer range. Because of mountains and wasteland on either hand, it was a gateway Coyle had to break through to get to the rich slope grass and nutritious white sage of the bottoms. It was the gap in a long natural barrier that Nick, and the four other riders in the outfit the slope ranchers had put up here, had to defend to the last.

When he let his horse slow down he grew aware of hoofs striking the earth hard and fast in the rear. He made a quick acceptance of the fact that the fight for his life still lay ahead and shuttled his eyes studiously over the forward country, which now slanted downward toward the deadline basin—Boulder. His horse was still fairly fresh, and his only chance was to ride for it.

Calmer than when he had left Carlita in the hot rocks, he put his horse to a steady gait. No cover showed itself before him, nothing but the seared brown plateau. He broke his gun and replaced the shell he had emptied in killing the dog. A moment later he saw three horsemen break over the rise behind, riding fast. He didn't shoot—they knew he would fight if they managed to close the gap.

From shape and dress, he had a strong hunch that the pursuers were Coyle and a couple of Boscos. The sheeper had a fine remuda, and the pursuers came on, strong and swift. Nick saw that he was barely holding his distance, and then it became certain that the others were gaining. His anxious glance probed across the foreground in another useless search for a place to make his stand.

Then he swore, brought his mount to a sliding

stop, whipped it around, knowing his best play was a fight on his own terms. The cowhorse under him made the turn, then went charging back as Nick began to shoot. He quartered a little from side to side, and saw the trio ahead pull apart in confusion. Bent low, he kept driving. His spaced, placed shots brought down a horse, its Basque rider going end over end into a cloud of dust. Tripp Coyle, a high, square shape in the saddle, ripped out some unintelligible order, then he and the intact Bosco dismounted hastily, shooting and trying to shield themselves behind their lunging horses.

Whipping his own mount about once again, Nick at last began to punish it. A crash of shots accompanied this action, and for a long breathless space he expected at any instant to feel the keen, hot bite of lead. When he looked back again, he saw they had given up taking him and were hunkered beside something revealed on the ground by the lifting dust. The downed Bosco had taken a hard fall.

An hour's riding brought Nick to the old Moccasin line camp that the deadline riders were using as headquarters. Quince Acton, whose turn it was to cook, was the only one there. An old man with the sour preoccupations of age, he came to the door and looked out as if he didn't quite see Nick.

"What them buzzards doing out there?" he asked finally.

Without answering immediately, Nick swung down, entered the soddy and walked to the coffee pot on the crane in the mud fireplace. Picking up a cup, he filled it from the pot's steaming contents and stared at the Dutch oven buried in the coals without actually seeing it.

Finally, with studied leisure, he said, "Breaking camp. They could be turning east the way we hoped they would after we warned 'em, but I don't think so. They're coming our way, Quince. Across the deadline, into the basin, then down the slope to the Short Line to ship their wool and lambs. All for free, except the freight, and on us." He made no mention of the fight he had had.

"They ain't going to do any part of that!" Quince said furiously. He had punched cattle on Snake Slope a long while—the land meant a great deal to him.

"They've got plenty of guns and men who can use 'em."

"They ain't bullet proof, are they?"

"Nor we." He said noncommittally, "Saw a couple of gents in their camp that ain't Boscos—and ain't sheepers."

He rolled a cigarette, lighted it and found no pleasure in its taste. Tall, dark and hard-fleshed, he controlled a fund of nervous energy with a stubborn, deadly mind—one reason he was bossing the present wrangle. He hadn't been able to choose the men with whom to hold the deadline against the sheep invasion, but had a blank check otherwise. Moccasin, for which he had ridden since losing his own ranch to sheepmen in an earlier war, Two Bar, Gooseneck, Wing I and Tin Cup were all represented by one man in the outfit. They were ranches that had fought in the first sheep war and lost, in that the fight had ended in an uneasy compromise. They would be the first on the slope to be invaded if Coyle broke through the gap.

Five years before the Snake and Humboldt cattlemen had been forced to acknowledge they could not keep sheep out of so vast a public domain. After bitter, useless fighting, an effort had been made to localize the woolies in areas not conflicting too much with cattle business. The arrangement had stopped the bloodshed, but had worked only in part, producing an uneasy, resentful peace. Now every sheepman let into the country at that time was watching Coyle, who was the pushing kind. One unjustified act on the part of a cowman would swing them instantly, hotly and solidly behind Coyle and his drifters, encouraging them to aggressions of their own and renewing hostilities throughout the region.

Except for that threat, which Coyle used callously, he could have been crushed easily, as he deserved to be. He was different from local sheepmen in his operation and in a way that made them look like stalwart citizens by contrast. Coyle bought cheap breeding ewes in California, often four or five bands of several thousand each, and trailed over the Sierras to winter around the Black Rock desert. After lambing in early spring, the flocks would drift on, feeding on stolen grass and leaving the trespassed range ruined for at least one whole season.

Grass pirates like Coyle never paid a nickel in taxes in the country they put to their own profit, or spent a dime for provisions if they could help. Drifting ever eastward, they would stop near some rail point at shearing time to ship wool and lambs. In late fall they would wind up in the Wyoming Basin where the breeders could be sold at twice their cost. The wool clip and lamb crop more than paid the paltry trail costs, while the money invested was often doubled. Guns lent their efficiency to cheap Basque labor, and the practice once started was hard to stop. It was too easy a way to get rich quick.

The other deadline riders came into the line camp together. Coyle kept his four flocks spread on a wide front so as to get enough grass, and Nick that morning had told the trio to check on them while he took a look at the main camp. The punchers were dusty, hot and patently excited. Andy Baggett, the big one, cracked his homely face in dry humor.

"Going to get us a dispute, maybe," he said. "Those woolies are all pointed the same way this morning. And moving."

"Our way?" Nick asked.

"So far." Andy had a red face that never tanned and a ropy mop of yellow hair. Out of his cherubic features came the shock of lethal eyes. In a soft voice, he said, "We rode in for orders, boss."

Bill Jarvis and Pace Erskine also wanted the answer for which Andy pressed. They were picked fighting men who so far had been kept from firing a hostile shot. The restraints of the touchy situation galled them, and with the detested sheep so close to their country their drive was strong. Sometimes they seemed to forget that Nick had lost a spread to sheepmen, and to mistake his hard-earned caution for uncertainty.

"No change in orders," Nick told them. His voice was flat, even, and he watched each man for a reaction. "We don't do a thing till Coyle crosses the deadline. You know why. If we hit him beforehand, we'll have a full-time war on our hands, the kind we lost once before. Every sheepman around here would pitch in behind Coyle. Coyle knows that. This time we'll take 'em as they come, one by one. This is a fight we got to win."

"Be damned," Bronco Bill Jarvis exploded,

"if I can tolerate it much longer. We know what he's going to do, and I say let's get in the first lick." A tall, dark man, he was a worry to Nick because of the unruliness of his nature that had got him nicknamed Bronco. He had come up from Gooseneck, always a hard-riding outfit, and wouldn't start for a halter much longer.

Pace Erskine, man of mystery, was different from the other two. Silent and secretive, he was a coldly courteous fellow of obvious education and as hard a man as ever punched cattle on the slope. A dark annoyance clouded his features but he said nothing. Nick watched Andy and Bronco shuttle a glance to each other. They had been holding a private conversation, he knew, and maybe had reached their own decision about things.

In a rough voice, Nick said, "Bronco, you stir up trouble and I'll send you down the slope a-packing. I mean that."

Bronco bristled, staring hard into Nick's eyes. He was a good hand, thoroughly dependable except for the wildness that was beginning to make him a name. But he seemed to see something in Nick that made him hold his tongue. With a shrug of his shoulders he walked away, Andy following.

Quince put foot on the table and let out his yell. Bronco and Andy both looked sulky when they came back from the barn. Pace Erskine's brown eyes were impassive. They ate in silence. Afterward Nick sent them out again to keep tabs on the sheep but with orders to stay out of sight. He wasn't sure what effect he had had when they rode out. Neither was Quince, who sourly began to wash up the dishes, a chore most punchers hated.

"Bronco's going to give you trouble," Quince reflected.

"Andy and Pace are just as ringy."

Quince agreed. "I wouldn't worry about Andy, except it's easy for a man like Bronco to lead him into trouble. But Pace has got more sense than both of 'em put together. Maybe he can keep 'em in hand. What you going to do this afternoon?"

"Ride over to Lilyville."

Quince frowned. "Bad place for you right now. Nothing but sheepers hang around there anymore, and now Coyle's men do."

"Which is why I'm going," Nick said. "Lily knows everybody and hears talk. If somebody's dropped something I ought to know, she'll tell me."

"Kind of got the inside track with her, ain't you?"

Nick said, "Lily's all right even if she is the only madam between the Snake and Humboldt."

"And about the only real woman a-tall," Quince reflected.

2

Lilyville's few adobe buildings straddled the Snake-Humboldt road. Originally there had been nothing but a roadhouse known as Lily's Place catering to the needs of cowhands from a few isolated ranches, prospectors from the high streams and rocky slopes, and travelers on the long and lonely road. With the establishment of sheep outfits in the vicinity, the settlement had added a store and blacksmith shop. Because of the strangely driven woman who had founded it, the town became Lily's town and finally was dignified by its permanent name. No one knew if this meant a thing to Lily Falcone.

Nick rode into the place in midafternoon, when the town seemed dead. He knew the deceptiveness of this, for the dark hours could see it a roaring hell of loosened passions and quick violence in which lonely men sought to escape the starved austerity of their lives. He racked his horse in front of Lily's, crossed the porch and entered her establishment.

She was alone in the bar. She looked up from the book she was reading, standing behind the high mahogany counter.

"If that plank was shorter," said Nick, "you could be a sky pilot delivering a sermon."

She laughed. "If this wasn't a house of ill repute."

"And gambling hell," Nick said amiably, "not to mention a damned good hotel."

"The usual?" Lily asked and lifted a bottle onto the bar, following it with a shot glass. Since the first one was on the house, Nick kept his money in his pocket and poured a drink. The woman watched him gravely out of the hidden experience of some thirty-five years, out of eyes gray and cool and distant except when a man knew her as he did.

What had been a striking beauty was still present in her though gray touched the edges of her auburn hair and a little bitterness lay at the ends of her mouth. Health and energy still filled the body that could have brought her wealth but had never been sold in this place. There was an amazing detachment in Lily toward the lowlife on which she lived—which was why she could stand it, Nick guessed.

Now she looked at him soberly. "I've got something for you, Nick—you can take it for what it's worth. A gunslinger of Coyle's let it drop that he's moving his sheep to Utah."

"Utah?" Nick said. "I take that for what it's worth."

"Which isn't much?"

"Which may be a lot. If Coyle was really drifting for Utah instead of crossing our way into

Idaho, he'd stay quiet to worry us. If he wanted a rumor like that spread, I'm glad I know. If he could get us to jump him, after him announcing that intention, we'd look mighty bad. And my boys are getting mighty hard to hold back. They're sure itching to shoot that outfit up."

Lily Falcone looked at him through a long moment. "You sound like the man in the middle. I'm afraid for you, Nick."

The door opened and a man came in. He looked at Nick, instantly truculent, then glanced at Lily.

"Kitty here?" he asked.

"In her room. Go on up, Frank."

The man turned toward the stairs and mounted them. "Early in the day," Nick reflected.

"They're going to get married. He's running sheep on Sand Creek. Being a cowboy, you'd say that for a sheepherder a tart's good enough."

"I'd say no such thing. For a sheepherder, Kitty is too damned good. Be seeing you, Lily."

"Make it soon."

Nick, as he rode out on the north road, knew he had gained from Lily everything she could tell him of Coyle's intentions. Actually he had hoped for something more tangible and his sense of foreboding was strong as Lilyville fell behind. He traveled fast.

The lifeless slopes of Boulder Basin seemed strange and lonely to him this year—always before the summer herds had been here at this time, with the cattle scattered across the graze and here and there some friendly puncher in sight for a man to stop and talk with. It had been decided not to bring up the cattle this year until the dispute with Coyle and his potential allies among the local sheep outfits had been settled. That was a precaution Nick considered wise, but one that galled a man's pride and was a drain on the graze farther down, which would be needed next winter.

He was moving into the boulder field of Thunderbird Canyon when his horse threw forward its ears and put its interest on the brushy area to the left of the trail. His first thought was that the animal might have scented a snake and he dropped a hand to the grip of his gun. A voice ripped out on the other side of the trail, "Easy, cowpoke! And make that gun hand scratch air!"

Nick turned slowly to see two men pace quietly toward him between the rocks to his right—both held guns on him. They were Canfield and Lacey, the two Coyle gunhands he had seen at the sheep camp that morning.

Thin and sandy-complexioned, Canfield had a hard mouth and a wedge of a jaw. His companion was runty but his stature only stressed the aggressive way he moved. Nick felt like a fool as he realized that they had hidden their horses on the opposite side of the trail, knowing his mount would sense the animals and divert its rider's attention in that direction, giving them the drop on him. His embarrassment must have shown on his face, because Canfield chuckled.

"Thought a cowpoke figured himself smarter'n a sheeper—but you sure looked the wrong way that time."

"You're no sheeper," Nick retorted. "You'd be my man if I offered you more than Coyle. What do you want?"

"Coyle hankers to see you. It's about that little business of shooting Carlita Corta's dog and then trying to force your way with her."

A brand-new anger took hold of Nick, an anger so deep it quieted him, like the wind will often die before a storm.

"I shot her dog," he said slowly, "to keep him from tearing me apart. All I done afterward was get out of there as fast as I could."

"That ain't what she says, Marquis. And Tripp Coyle sure don't like a man trying to breach his fences, especially a cowman."

Nick fought down the urge to bring his hand down in one wild stab for his gun. It didn't matter that the girl had lied about what happened between them that morning—what roiled in Nick was that the story would be believed. It was the kind of thing many men liked to believe, and let a report such as Canfield had just hinted at drift across the sheep country and all hell would break loose.

Canfield, perhaps divining with a gunman's acumen, Nick's nearness to an explosion, moved up to Nick quickly, reached and took Nick's gun from its holster. He stepped back. His gunhawk's vanity was still gratified by the easy capture and his eyes danced. He nodded to Lacey, who slipped off among the rocks across the trail. Presently the little man returned, mounted and leading another horse. Canfield swung to saddle. He pointed.

"Lead the way, Marquis," he said curtly. "And don't forget there's plenty of reasons you should be dead."

Nick swung his horse and rode stolidly while it climbed out of the rocky draw. His mind ran swiftly over the situation. He knew his own total jeopardy—but whatever happened to him, his riders would have the excuse they wanted to start shooting.

Escape, for the moment, seemed out of the question. If he tried to break and ride for it, his captors would drop him out of the saddle, and the story of an attempted attack on the Basque girl would justify them in many quarters. Not all cowmen would believe the claim, but every sheeper in the country would accept and back it to the limit. He rode cursing the girl—and himself for having let her surprise him watching Coyle's camp. He could almost understand her side of it—a Bosco loved a dog.

They were riding now against the lowering sun,

its white glare blanching the slopes and making Nick keep his eyes to the ground. They had moved across the upper edge of Boulder when the sun dropped behind the higher hills.

Nick realized from their general direction that Coyle had moved his camp on an eastward course, contrary to what Nick had guessed of his intentions that morning. He was still well back from the deadline, moving toward Utah and not Snake Slope, as the planted rumor had claimed he intended. The supposed assault on the girl was just the extra touch Coyle had needed. It made the tramp sheepers look completely innocent of guile, and one Nick Marquis completely off the track.

They passed one of the flocks as they rode, a loose band feeding quietly. Two men guarded it, one a Bosco foot herder handling the sheep with the help of a dog, the other mounted and armed. Both Basques lay a searching glance on the riders but, apparently recognizing Canfield and Lacey, showed no alarm. A little later the new sheep camp showed below in a hollow.

To Nick's surprise, neither Coyle nor Carlita was in evidence when the gunmen rode in with their captive. A swarthy humpbacked Basque was busy cooking, with a couple of others loafing about.

"Where's Tripp?" Canfield called to the *cocinero*.

The man shrugged and pointed in what would be the general direction of Lilyville and the sheep layouts around there. Nick's mouth pulled into a hard twist—Coyle would be busy spreading the rumor about him and Carlita Corta and trying to line up help for his final plans.

At Canfield's bidding, Nick swung down. Lacey caught the reins of his and Canfield's horses and took the animals out to the picket line.

"Might as well find a seat, Marquis," said Canfield. "You're going to be here a while."

Nick saw no advantage in the fact that they didn't rope him. There were five armed men in and about the camp, and while they seemed indifferent their attention never completely left him. One by one the others ate, but nobody invited Nick to partake of what he knew, with aversion, to be mutton. His hunger hardly registered—all his thoughts and feelings were, for the moment, focused on escape before his own men organized a rescue attempt that would trigger a full-scale range war.

Long after nightfall a party of four rode in. Not until they had come into the light of the campfire, dismounted and turned their horses over to the waiting wrangler, was Nick sure they were Coyle and Carlita, with two Basque men whose excitement at recognition of the prisoner was even more marked than Coyle's.

Tripp Coyle was a craggy man of notably

solid build. Although his weathered face was of indeterminate age, he was probably still short of the middle years. Staring into the man's gleaming eyes, Nick wondered at the man's attraction for a girl like Carlita, who for some reason, failed to share her companions' interest in the captive.

"You get it set up in Lilyville?" Canfield asked.

"It's all set." Tripp Coyle glanced at the Basques who had arrived with him. "Well, boys, it was your sister he roughed up, and I promised you the pleasure of working him over."

Nick had heard of Carlita's brothers, Pilar and Tomas, who were reported to be lesser partners with Coyle in the grass stealing venture. They were handsome men, tall and dark, and their eyes held the sheen of pure hatred. It grew plain that Carlita had lied, for they seemed really to believe that he had abused her.

"Only one thing wrong about that," Nick drawled. "I never touched the *señorita* or tried or even wanted to, and she knows it. Let her look me in the eye and claim otherwise."

Carlita tossed her head, and he knew she was remembering the shot he had drilled into her dog. But suddenly she whirled a look at Coyle and cried, "Tripp Coyle, I will not have this! He kill my King, but I did not say—"

"Shut up!" Coyle snapped.

Both Corta men seemed astonished. Then there began between them and the girl a swift, fluid flow of talk that meant nothing to Nick. The men lost their surprise and seemed angered, but she got in the last word, some sharp command, and the brothers shrugged in submission.

Turning back to Nick, the girl said, "It makes little difference, but you should know it was not I who made up the lie. And it is not necessary that my brothers believe it and kill you in the manner they intended. That is why I changed my mind—not that I am sorry for you."

Nick felt aversion sweep up his back. The fact that her brothers might not kill him "in the manner they had intended" promised him little. A Bosco was a devil with a knife, and the brothers' threat remained, particularly if the rest of the sheepmen thought he had violated the girl.

"She's right," Coyle rapped out. "It makes no difference now. Once them goaty punchers from the basin take a swipe at us, the part about her won't matter."

"I do not like to be made the fool of, Tripp Coyle," Pilar Corta murmured. "I do not like to have my sister's name used for such a reason. It will not happen again."

The three Cortas walked off toward the remuda.

"All right, Coyle," Nick said softly. "You've still got it lined up neat, but let me warn you. All the help you can get hereabouts won't let you take your woolies across the slope. You'll lose them short of the railroad, and God knows how many men you'll get killed."

Coyle laughed silently. "I'll move my sheep where I want, and no damned cowman's going to dictate to me. Come on, boys. Let's get this job done."

Nick spun and struck out at the man he had sensed to be moving up behind him. His fist landed solidly in the belly of Canfield, who gushed air and bent over. Nick kicked him in the face but somebody landed on his back before he could reach Canfield's gun and took him down hard.

He rolled, using his spurred boots and elbows on the man at his back, and managed to break clear and get to his feet. Men were running at him from all sides. He met them as they came, his fists going like battering rams, feeling the shirt ripped from his body, taking a staggering rain of blows.

Somebody drove head on at him and Nick, placing his hands on the fellow's shoulders, leaped over him. This put him momentarily at the edge of the melee, which gain he used to make a break for the horses. Then something sailing through the air smashed against the back of his head and he went down. A great roar assailed his ears, and suddenly he knew nothing.

3

Something kept pounding him in the belly, brutally, endlessly. The roaring still filled his ears, and his head seemed on the point of falling off. It took him a long time to figure out that he was tied face down across a saddle. Later this fact grew into a realization that he was being taken somewhere away from the sheep camp. He thought vaguely of men who had disappeared in the other sheep war, their carrioned-off skeletons found long afterward in some lonely canyon.

He never wholly lost consciousness, after that, though he had neither sight nor sound of his captors. He knew he had absorbed a terrible beating, to which had been added the concussing impact of what might have been a bullet or a thrown object, a pistol or a rock. Then all at once men were shouting, and he was being loosened from the saddle and taken into somebody's arms.

"The dirty devils!" a man said bitterly at what seemed a great distance. "Beat him senseless, tied him to his saddle and sent his horse home!"

He thought the voice was Bronco Bill's but wasn't sure for the black curtain came down again.

He awakened with a clear but aching head to find himself in his bunk at the Moccasin line camp. Quince Acton was seated in the chair across from him, lost in sour thoughts. The camp was strangely silent.

"Where're the boys?" Nick rasped.

Quince shoved up quickly and strode over. He wore a deeply anxious expression. It dawned on Nick that daylight had come, so his second lapse into unconsciousness must have lasted several hours.

Quince said, "I give you one guess as to that."

"Damn 'em!" Nick said. "They couldn't wait for me to tell 'em what happened before going after Coyle, huh?"

"That's what they had on their minds when they left. I couldn't talk 'em out of it. They could pretty well figure what had happened from the way you looked. So could I."

Nick shoved to a sitting position. His face throbbed and when he put a hand to it he felt rough bandages. His whole body ached. "Got to stop them, Quince!" he said drunkenly. "That's all Coyle wanted. He's going to blame the beating I got on Carlita's brothers and the other Basques and claim that we attacked his sheep without a reason." Swiftly he outlined the story Coyle was circulating about himself and the Basque girl.

"You just take it easy. They done a mean beat-up on you, and moving around right now could be dangerous," Quince advised. "If the boys happen to down Coyle things may not get too bad."

"The hell with that! Coyle's been taking care of himself too long to slip up now!" Somehow Nick got his feet on the floor. The room spun and dipped. When it stopped he managed to weave himself erect.

"Now you've come to," Quince was saying, "I can go after them. I'll see if I can stop 'em."

"No, I've got to go. If they wouldn't listen to you the first time, they won't now."

"I'll sure go with you, though," Quince said.

Nick had little hope that disaster could be averted. Quince told him that Bronco, Andy and Pace had left as soon as they were sure he was going to live. Anything could have happened by now, for Coyle had been ready for a reprisal and had probably set a trap.

Nick had trouble getting into the saddle and hanging on afterwards. Fortunately, after the first few hundred yards they had to slow to look for sign.

After a long while, Quince said, "What I don't see is why they didn't beef you when they had the chance."

"They licked us once in open war—Coyle's playing for that again. He might have trouble getting the backing of the local sheepmen if the first killing came from his side."

The sun was well over the horizon, building to its full incandescence and heat. The sign left by the three enraged punchers pointed north of Coyle's camp, probably to one of the sheep bands.

Long before he expected it, Nick heard the rattle of distant gunfire. Reining in, he placed the sound to the right of their course.

"What the hell?" Quince barked, his face going slack.

"We'll find out. Come on."

Juniper dotted the distant rise toward which they spurred, and beyond it a clean line of rimrock slashed across the hot sky. Plunging through the stand of stunted trees, they could see a little below them another of the region's countless crops of rock. If this were the scene of the fight, it was well away from the sheep camp and flocks, and something was terribly wrong. His men could not have started anything here that would have harmed Coyle.

Quince was already figuring it out. He said, "Ten to one they romped into more than they could handle, then got chased back and nailed down over there. In a way, it serves them wild Injuns right."

"We'll have to move in on them quiet," Nick reflected. "It's our only chance to help."

They bent their course toward the *bajada* rising slowly to the right of the source of the steady, angry shots. In this wise the ground swell kept them covered until they were in the big outwash of rock and gravel from the eroding rimrock. The gunfire's beat was sharp and jarring, interpierced by the scream of bullets glancing off the rocks. Nick swung out of leather and bellied up the slope Injun style.

He reached a point where he could get his first real look at the situation. To his right, puffs of powdersmoke pinpointed the fighters—then, some distance away, he spotted three basin horses. His riders, closely pursued, had been forced to head for this rock field, quit their horses and take cover. From what he could judge, Nick suspected that the pursuing sheepers had cut the cowboys off from their mounts. The three deadline riders were in a fight for their lives and apparently had been for several hours.

Whispering, Nick said, "From what I saw, Coyle's got eight or nine fighting men. We can't hope to beat them. Best we can do is come in behind and open a way for the boys to pull out. You ready?"

Quince nodded, and Nick turned and made a crouching run to the next concealing rock. He had his gun out and his eyes slid and probed across the rocks ahead and below him. He had made several forward, zigzag runs before he saw stretched out, at a slightly lower level, the body of a man. Since the gaudy shirt did not look familiar, the other was probably a sheepman, but Nick wasn't sure enough to shoot. There was only one alternative; he moved on in.

Step by slow step he came closer, the crackling gunfire covering the small sounds he could not help making. The fellow heard him in the last second and twisted a swarthy head toward Nick, then was smashed flat by the impact of Nick's body. He made a gagging grunt before Nick shoved the sweating dark face into the dirt to prevent an outcry. A rap of the gun barrel, and the figure was wholly inert. Nick shoved to a hunker, panting, his eyes darting right and left.

He had for the time being drawn upon some deep source of energy that wiped away his recent exhaustion. If he and Quince could clear this side, he could call to his men to make a running fight in this direction. He had lost track of Quince, but there was no firing immediately about him.

A moment's listening, then Nick prowled on. The heat of the rock rolled about him and sweat stung his eyes and his bandaged face and head.

Finally he caught sight of a man he recognized. Pilar Corta had crawled in close to the firing line. He held a Winchester, and his flashing eyes prospected the foreground hungrily. He was turned a quarter away from Nick, and the gap between the two was wide. Nick wanted the man with a desperate longing but knew that if he called out he might invite a shot from some hidden quarter. Once more he began his catlike prowl, feeling and placing each foot carefully while his intent gaze never left the Basque. All at once, as if warned by some animal faculty, Corta swung himself and the rifle. But Nick's pistol had him covered.

"Don't try it, Pilar!" he hissed. "You can't make it!"

Pilar Corta's jaw thrust out belligerently, and the dark eyes flashed a wicked defiance, a swirling challenge. But he saw the gun in the cowman's hand, and he saw death in the eyes that held his own. Action died in the supple body, and Pilar shrugged.

Nick made a beckoning motion that at first Pilar ignored. What the Basque saw in the man commanding him started him crawling then, toward Nick, leaving the rifle on the hot ground. When the Bosco had reached him, Nick motioned for him to keep on, moving back farther into the protecting rocks.

"You are one tough *señor, si?*" Pilar panted.

"You'll be a dead *señor*, you give me trouble."

For the moment they were in safe cover from the crisscrossing bullets. Pilar had a knife in his belt but no handgun, and Nick reached cautiously and took the knife. That accomplished, Nick shouted at the top of his voice.

"Coyle! It's Marquis, and you'd better listen!"

The shooting died like fire under a pail of water. In the strangely oppressive silence that followed, Coyle answered uncertainly.

"Who?"

"Nick Marquis, and I've got your girlfriend's brother—Pilar. I don't reckon she'd like it if you let something happen to him."

"You're lying," Coyle returned. "Pilar, where are you?"

"Tell him," Nick ordered the Basque. "In the best English you can muster, and no tricks."

Defiance rose in the eyes of Pilar and died away. "It is so, Tripp!" he called. "The *vaquero* he means business!"

After a long moment, Coyle yelled, "All right, Marquis, what's the offer?"

"Let my men come out to me without a fuss."

"Then you'll turn Pilar loose?"

"I never said that. But I'm saying he's one dead sheepherder if I don't see my men real quick, in which case Carlita is likely to kick you out of her sheep wagon."

Pilar let out a growl and for a moment seemed about to defy the gun and spring at Nick. Then he subsided, but his eyes flashed hate. "For that, *señor*," he panted, "I will some day cut out your tongue!"

"Not today, you won't."

Tripp Coyle seemed to have a hard time making up his mind. Finally the order Nick hardly expected to hear rang out.

"Let them go, boys. We got what we wanted from 'em already."

"Make for your horses!" Nick called to his

surrounded men. "I'm holding onto this ringy Bosco for insurance!"

Quince appeared out of the rocks, and his wry face for once wore a grin. But the look he gave Pilar held pure murder, and the Basque obeyed quietly when Nick motioned for him to move out, away from the others. Nick fell in behind, with Quince bringing up the rear.

Out on the edge of the sun-seared rock field they waited until Andy appeared, then Pace and Bronco Bill. Nick emitted a sigh of relief at seeing them all on their feet, apparently unhurt. They wore sheepish looks, but there was no time to waste here, and they moved together at a hurried gait toward the distant horses.

"Tripp Coyle has kept the bargain," Pilar said, then. "I go back."

"You're coming with us, Corta," Nick snapped.

"But I have no horse."

"Got a pair of legs, ain't you?" Quince growled.

The legs of Pilar Corta had been made into spring steel by his lifetime as a walking shepherd. He had no trouble staying ahead of the moving horses as the cowmen rode down toward Boulder Basin.

"Sure you ain't making a mistake holding onto him?" Quince asked finally.

"We've all done nothing but play into Coyle's hands up to now," Nick rasped. "One more mistake won't hurt none."

"Hell, boss," Andy said uneasily, "we just couldn't set on our hind ends after what that sheeper done to you."

"What good did getting yourselves treed do anybody?"

An embarrassed grin broke the dogged look on the face of Bronco Bill. "Getting treed wasn't our idea. That man sure had things ready for us. We only got to pop a few shots into that sheep band at Sweet Springs and, Lord A'mighty! A dozen men were on top of us, and God knows where they come from."

"You killed some sheep outside the deadline?"

"Hit a few, thank God."

"Well, man," Nick said hotly, "the whole Snake Slope is going to help you pay for them!"

Two hours later they reached the Moccasin line camp. Although he had covered several miles at his walking trot, Pilar Corta showed no signs of wear beyond a film of dust and sweat. Nick swung out of saddle and motioned to the Basque to go into the soddy's cooler interior. At his nod, the other punchers rode on to take care of the horses. Nick stepped into the house behind Corta.

Pointing to the water pail, he said, "Help yourself."

Pilar seemed surprised at the consideration. Then, moving catlike across the room, he dipped water and drank thirstily. He wiped the sleeve of his shirt across his mouth. Nick told him to sit down, took the chair across the table, and pulled out tobacco and papers. Pilar again showed astonishment when he was offered the makings. He shook his head.

"I made a mistake about your sister," said Nick. "Shouldn't have used her name. Only did it because she made me sore, and I wondered if Coyle might not think more of her than of you."

"That will not be forgotten, *vaquero*."

"You're wondering why I brought you here. Not to beat you up, Corta. Maybe Coyle's the one who spread the yarn that I tried to attack your sister, but she let him do it. You don't have to tell me why—she not only hates me for killing her dog, but you people want to get the plateau sheepmen to come in with you and fight us. And that was a good way to make certain they would."

"This kind of talk is suppose' to do some good?" Pilar asked scornfully.

"Maybe not. Just the same, after she told you the truth, you and your brother didn't want any part of beating me up. I put that on the credit side of the books. I have a hope, Pilar, that if the local sheepmen heard the truth about that, they wouldn't let Coyle use them, either."

"Who is to tell them the truth?" Pilar asked.

"You."

"Or I get kill'?"

"No," Nick said. "I'm just asking you to do it."

"You are the very strange *hombre*," Pilar

reflected. "Coyle think he has put you out of business, but you come and spoil the nice fight. Jus' the same, I do not like you. Even if you kill me, I will not help save you from Tripp Coyle."

"Save me?" Nick said with a laugh. "Man, you seem to have confidence in that fellow."

"Coyle will avenge the death of our father, Jesus Corta, who never harmed any man. He has sworn it, *vaquero*. He will take land from the cowmen and give it to us for the land we lost."

In his proud defiance, Pilar might not have realized how much he conveyed in that boast. Taking land from the cowmen? That suggested plans in Coyle's mind Nick had not suspected. Coming forward in the chair, he said, "You pack a load of hate, Pilar. What happened to you—and Carlita, since she seems to feel the same way?"

A sudden passion twisted the dark features of the man.

"Once, *señor*," he said in a low, embittered voice, "we have the little *rancho* in the high hills where we harm nobody. We have the house with the blue walls and the music and dancing. We play the pelota an' watch the shepherds' fires on the hills in the night. It is beautiful. Then one day comes a man, a cattle king—and it is finish'. Our father, Jesus Corta, is burn', tied to the wheel of his wagon. Our sister is made to dance without the clothes for this cattle king. He is no longer living, *vaquero*. I, Pilar Corta, saw to that."

A sadness lay deep in Nick all at once. His own voice lowered, he said, "It's a two-sided row, Pilar. Cowmen have got their stories, too, none nice listening. It happens I lost a cattle ranch to the sheepers already in this country. Does that surprise you?"

"It is of no importance. We collect now what is due."

"How?"

Pilar smiled. "You think I tell you, Nick Marquis?"

Stepping outside, Nick saw his four riders hunkered in the shade of the little barn. Except for Quince, they gave him a quick, uneasy glance as he strode toward them.

Curtly, Nick said, "I warned you men. Everybody but Quince can roll up his blankets and go home."

The three besides Quince came to their feet, mouths open, eyes disbelieving.

"My God, Nick!" Andy gasped. "It was only because of you we went up there!"

"And it'll be because of you the whole sheep country'll swing behind Coyle. Our only chance of handling him without filling the creeks with blood was to keep them out of it. I told you that a dozen times, and it didn't mean a thing when you got exercised. I'm not risking any more of that."

"You and Quince can't stand off Coyle when he

comes to get Corta," Bronco said, still stunned. "Which he will, sure as shooting."

"We'll stand him off till your outfits can get replacements up here. Go on, now. Roll your beds and ride."

They were good men, of the best, and he hated to lose them. Putting his flat stare from face to shocked face, he saw that they knew he was right. Bronco sent a desperate look to the other two. Then, squaring his shoulders, he looked back at Nick.

"It's my fault, not theirs. I done the egging on. If I'd kept my big mouth shut, they'd have listened to Quince. I got it coming, and I'll ride, but I hate to see Andy and Pace get it, too."

Looking up from his bunker, Quince said, "I don't reckon they'd do it again, Nick. And they ought to have a chance to help clean up the mess."

After a scowling moment, Nick said, "All right," and turned.

4

Nick bathed his mauled body in cool creek water, taking some of the feverishness out of his flesh. In clean clothes from his war bag he felt better, although the level of his energy was below par. He had started Quince and Pace down the slope an hour ago, with Pilar. Holding the Bosco as hostage was the only way left to check Coyle until the slope ranchers could muster the fighting force Nick had been forced to call for.

By moving Corta out of the country at once, the danger of an attempt by the sheepmen to free him was greatly lessened. It left only three riders on the deadline, but all five could not have held the line if Coyle were to make a real effort to breach it.

The sun was by then only two or three hours above the red-tinged horizon. Nick was thinking as he walked back to camp that it might not be well for them to spend the night there. Andy and Bronco were smoking their after-supper cigarettes on the shady side of the soddy. They avoided looking directly at Nick as he came back.

"I'm riding over to Lilyville," Nick told them, "to see what effect all this has had. After dark you boys take your blankets into the hills to sleep. That Bosco outfit might make a pass at this camp now that they've got an excuse."

Bronco said somberly, "Good idea. Next time I tangle with them sons I don't want to be pinned down if I can help it. And you better watch your-own-self—from what's been said about you around Lilyville, them sheepers might try to string you up."

"Trying and doing are different things," Nick answered. "I'll meet you at Chimney Rock at noon tomorrow. If the sheepers make a try for you, learn what you can, but don't do any shooting you don't have to do."

He saddled a fresh horse and rode off with the evening shadows lengthening and the bright, piercing heat gone out of the day. His nerves loosened and he felt better. He hoped Coyle was too drawn to Carlita to take action endangering the life of her brother. That would buy a little time, and Nick had to gamble on its being enough for strong reinforcements to reach him at Boulder Basin. His one hope left of avoiding a flaming range war was a quick show of strength by the cowmen, which might keep the other sheepmen from joining Coyle in spite of their outraged feelings.

He knew it would be foolish to show himself openly in town at present and turned into the stunted pine on the last downslope, loosened the cinch of his saddle and stretched out to rest and kill time. Almost at once he was asleep.

When he awoke, the wheeling stars told him it was around midnight. Lilyville would just about now be hitting full stride. He tightened the latigo, swung up and went on. A little later he rode in toward the back door of the stable behind Lily's place. Passing through, he quietly put up his horse. Another back door let him into the roadhouse, where he climbed a pair of service stairs to the second floor.

Kitty Breckenridge was alone in her room when he knocked. She was dark and small and, like all of Lily's girls, sedate enough in manner. She gave Nick a startled glance, then beckoned him hastily into the room and shut the door.

"You're a fool to come here!" she breathed.

"I hear you're going to marry a sheepherder," Nick said, grinning at her through the lamplight. "But I still trust you, Kitty. Tell Lily I'm here, will you?"

"This place is packed with sheepmen!" Kitty said, her eyes moving nervously over his bruised face. "Including some of Coyle's men. They had a general meeting tonight."

"So?" Nick said with interest. "What did they decide?"

"Even if I knew I wouldn't tell you. Nick, I do like you, though. You'd better go up to that room on the third floor. It's hot but safe. I'll tell Lily."

"Fine."

Stepping out to the hall again, Nick took the stairs to the ovenlike top floor of the place. What Kitty had said about a sheepmen's meeting made him glad he had risked this visit. He entered the upper bedroom, which was used only when Lily's accommodations were strained, walked hastily to the window and opened it to let in cooler air. He could see the crowded street now, horses along the hitchrails and a couple of buggies.

Almost at once there was a low rap on the door and, when he opened it, Lily Falcone slipped into the room. She closed the door carefully.

"You idiot," she breathed. "Don't you know you're practically asking to be killed?"

"Not exactly—what I am asking for is information." Nick grinned. "Do you know what went on at that sheep meeting?"

"They took up the question of continuous outrages against the sheep interests. Things got pretty hot. They voted to back Coyle straight down the line."

"Well, that's no surprise," Nick reflected. "Was he there?"

She shook her head. "He didn't need to be after the story he spread about you yesterday."

"Me and the Basque girl? Did you believe it?"

"Of course not," Lily returned. "And a lot of others wouldn't if they weren't hunting an excuse to take up the old quarrel. That's all I can tell you, so far, and I better not stay. Where's your horse?"

"In your barn."

"That's all right," she decided. "Anybody who knows me knows better than to poke into my affairs. For which reason you'd better go down to my room. It's cooler than this one, too."

"Didn't figure to stay, Lily."

"There's no safer place for you right now, and I might hear more before that hot-headed bunch downstairs breaks up." Without waiting to let him protest again, the woman turned and was gone.

Nick knew the way to the private quarters of Lily Falcone, which were in a back wing and as far removed from the hubbub of her business as she could get. Listening carefully each time he moved, he made his way down the back stairs. Outside, he stood for a moment looking toward the barn, still weighing the wisdom of getting his horse and heading into the hills. Yet she was right. She might learn more tonight, and all he could do otherwise was hide out until morning. He turned toward her door, which he found unlocked.

It was a pleasant room, cross-ventilated, and he felt at once its refreshing coolness. Moving through the darkness to one of its easy chairs, he took seat and his fingers shaped a cigarette. Lighting up, he smoked as he considered how readily the local sheepmen had thrown in with the itinerant band of Coyle. What Lily had said about their only needing an excuse summed it up. When he finished the cigarette he pulled off his boots and stretched out on the couch. Another night and where might he be sleeping, he wondered. It could well be underground.

He didn't awaken until he felt Lily shaking him. Opening his eyes, he saw her bending over him.

"Anything new?" he asked drowsily.

"No, except that the more they drink the more they want a fight. Nick, I hate it. I spent so many years among cowmen that when the sheepmen took over around here I wanted to sell out. Before long I was glad I stayed. Most of them are just like you people, fighting this hard country, trying to wring a living from it. Coyle's using them, and I've said so straight out. But they're too inflamed to listen."

"If you're through for the night," Nick reflected, "you'd want your quarters. I'll be off."

"You'd better wait till daylight and not risk running into one of them. I've got a separate bedroom—with a lock on the door." She grinned at him and walked away.

Nick heard a door open and close. A little later he thought he heard the soft snick of a key in the lock, and grinned. By God, she'd meant it!

It was lighter than he liked when at last he saddled his horse. Yet a cautious look along the street showed him that Lilyville was once more deserted. He led the horse out into the open, swung up. Soon he was safely away from the little town.

Around eleven o'clock he drew near Chimney Rock. The rock stood at the rim of an eminence that let a man have a good look at the country. Mounting it, Nick turned his brooding attention to the southwest. Out there somewhere Coyle was waiting to make the next move in his deadly game, yet he saw no movement now.

His cynical, merciless game. Nick wondered if the Lilyville sheepmen remotely wondered if they weren't being used—as Lily had told them—if even the nomadic Basques did not, sometimes. Coyle was not and would never be a champion of the Corta cause, or of any other. A man of his cut never planned a move not based on cold, calculating self-interest.

It was just at noon when Nick saw the two riders coming toward him from the north. Andy and Bill rode into the shadow below the rim.

"Any trouble?" Nick asked.

"No trouble," Bill answered. "But we're sure starved. Figure it's safe for us to go to camp and rustle some grub?"

"We'll take a look."

They rode east. The line camp was tranquil and showed no sign of having been bothered in the night. They fixed a meal and ate it.

"When do you reckon we'll get help, Nick?" Andy asked.

"Be another day."

"I hope Coyle don't decide his fat profits look better than the Corta girl. She must be holding him back on account of her brother. But if he's got the high country sheepers riled up, he might have to act pronto, regardless of what might happen to Pilar. Sometimes a man can start something he can't stop. I sure found that out."

All at once the three men were listening with hard interest to a distant, loudening sound. A horse was coming on fast from down the slope.

"That's Pace's blaze horse!" Andy breathed. "And Pace is sure covering ground!"

Nick felt a quick alarm rise in him. Pace Erskine wheeled up in front of the line camp, and his hard eyes held a smoky light. "Corta got away," he said tiredly. "I never saw a man do what that Bosco did and live. On that shelf road above Myers Creek—he jumped off, horse and all, and made it. The water washed them out of sight before we could get in a shot. Pulled out downstream and hit for the sheep camp. The way the banks were we couldn't get across to chase him before he was gone."

"There goes our arm-twist on Coyle," Andy said dismally.

"Where's Quince?" Nick asked Pace.

"Went on for reinforcements. We thought I'd better get back here quick."

The news shocked Nick. The shelf road above Myers Creek was high, and nobody would have expected action as utterly reckless as the one Pilar had taken. The Basque had taken an enormous gamble, but he had made it, and now nothing stood in the way of Coyle's invasion.

"What are we going to do?" Bill asked, voicing the question crowding for an answer in Nick's own mind. "Let him come into the basin and wait till we get enough help to wipe him out?"

Nick shook his head. "We do what we came up here to do. We stand on the deadline. When it's crossed, we fight."

Oddly, though they must have known how desperate the fight would be, he saw their spirits lift and watched excitement stir violently through them. When Coyle came into Boulder Basin, his flocks would be moving on a wide front, each under guard. He was so well situated he could use every device of deception and force. He could not be met head-on, and now Nick examined some of the plans he had made against this time.

The herders and armed guards assigned to the four bands would have all they could do moving and protecting their flocks. Coyle's extra gunfighters, the Corta brothers and the general camp tenders, were free to move where needed and would be Coyle's main strength. If they could be held in check, the deadline riders might be able to turn back the sheep themselves. A little riding and shooting around a band would soon make it unmanageable.

Nick said, "We'd best scatter out. The question's how he's going to use his fighters and what we can do to offset them. Each of us keeps moving and covers his stretch of ground. There's one thing that might pay off. Coyle knows we'll have help soon. He's relying on the threat of the other sheepers coming in if our side gets too hostile. We've got to show those Lilyville people Coyle isn't as powerful as he's made them think. Then they might wonder if they want to bet all they've gained here on a man of his kind."

"How are we going to do that?" Bronco asked.

"One way," Pace put in, "is to make the kind of fool of him he made of us three."

"That's sort of the idea," Nick agreed. "You boys get out on the deadline, and you'll have to take a third of it each until I can get there, too. A sheep don't stampede the way a steer does, but it's easy to turn one senseless. The Boscos with the bands know that and that we'll have to be dealt with before they dare risk all that wool and mutton. It's my hunch they'll rely on Coyle and a riding party to handle us."

"What are we going to do to that riding party?" Pace inquired.

"Leave it to me. You get on up there and watch

the sheep. Raise all the hell possible if they head our way. I'll try to keep Coyle's wolf pack tangled up."

The others saddled again and rode out. Nick was soon mounted and heading southwest toward the tramp sheeper's camp. He felt very lonely but he rode at a steady pound.

5

Heat lay thick and dry about him when he neared the deadline edge of Boulder Basin. As he traveled his mind turned backward to the little spread he had once owned on Christmas Creek, east of Lilyville, and the herd he had built under his own iron, struggling for the competence any hardworking man had a right to expect. At first he had liked the remoteness here, but the marginal location had been his and several others' undoing.

He had never held it against the cattlemen that his had been one of the ranches sacrificed to the crowding sheepmen in the compromise that had brought a truce but no peace to the range, that his steers had been killed or run off in the fighting. Such adjustments were being made everywhere in the cattle country now that the sheep business had grown powerful in its own right. But he missed the spread and, although he had found a good job on Moccasin, he never got over resenting his loss.

Now that he had done everything possible to stop another war, his conscience was clear. He did not deceive himself about the mounting excitement in him, a hunger for vengeance, a chance to strike again at the faction that had cost him so dearly. Right or wrong, a man's hatred was not something he could quickly dislodge.

An hour later he was on Dead Squaw Butte, from where he could see the sheep camp. It showed no signs of intending to move, but he had not expected that it would. The thing that interested him, as he adjusted his vision to the glare of the sun, was that most of Coyle's nomadic hirelings were still there. The sheep outfit was still making preparations and so far no Lilyville men had joined it.

Nick had left his horse hidden on the blind side of the rise and he carried a Winchester. Lifting the piece to his shoulder, he took careful aim at the camp and deliberately squeezed the trigger, enjoying the slam of the butt against his shoulder. He grinned as the men in camp dived for cover. He fired again—then, showing himself openly, temptingly, he sprinted back across the rise to his horse.

Again in the leather, he swung the mount sharply, making for a low bench. He knew this country well. Shortly he dismounted and led the horse up the *bajada* and on through a notch to the top. With the rim cutting him from sight, he again trailed reins and left the animal. He dropped flat to the edge of the blistering rock, removing his hat so as not to expose himself too plainly. The heat soon had him sweating profusely.

He had begun to think that Coyle didn't consider a lone enemy worth bothering with, when suddenly he saw two riders break into sight on top of the butte. They were Canfield and Lacey, feeling their way cautiously. For a moment they studied the sign he had left, and he saw them swing to follow it along the course he had taken. He let them come within rifle range, then fired twice, as rapidly as he could jack the piece and trigger it. He saw the two horses go down, the riders sprawling. Nick followed the scrambling gunmen with lead until they had gained cover behind the threshing bodies of the horses. He reflected with vengeful satisfaction that he could have killed them both had he not wanted more action out of them.

He got it; the two gunmen began to shoot back in savage earnestness. But they were using their handguns and he could hear the bullets die aimlessly in the rock below him. He kept his carbine going just enough to keep them firing. The rattle of the exploded powder crackled along the rim. He wondered how long it would be before uneasy curiosity brought others to investigate.

Already Coyle would be worried, wondering if this attack had been made to pin down his main fighting force while another assault was made on his sheep. This fear would force him to disperse his men for the sheep's protection, robbing him of the initiative. A savage desire for vengeance riding him now, Nick ignored the heat that wrapped about him from the rock and poured down from a molten sky.

In this painful, self-imposed entrapment, it seemed a long while before he realized that the shooting had brought others out. A man's figure revealed itself for an instant on the sun-blanched top of the butte across from him, then drew back hastily. A little later he thought that he saw three men over there, flattened now and studying the area below them.

He knew he had forced on them a real and urgent problem. The gunmen pinned down behind the dead horses, there in the open, were Coyle's best fighters. They could not retreat, nor was there any way they could be rescued without a long and tedious struggle. No one could get on top of the mesa, Nick knew from experience, except by the way he had chosen and which he could cover with the rifle.

Conversely, he could not himself get down now. This condition he had accepted readily in his determination to tie Coyle up until a fighting force could arrive from the cattle ranges. But the heat of the rock was more punishing than his fear of being captured by the sheepmen again, and before long a rasping thirst tormented him.

He had extra shells in his pocket and had hoped that Canfield and Lacey would in their first flash of anger spend their ammunition, but the lessened shooting from the other side meant Coyle's hired guns were wasting no more lead than was necessary to immobilize him.

At long last heat stupor began to get Nick. He began to realize he couldn't take much more of this. At last he shoved himself backward from the edge of the rim and turned to see his droop-necked horse waiting in painful obedience. The animal's suffering, as much as his own, decided him.

He swayed for a moment after he pushed himself erect. Then, leading the horse, he started back down. All at once shade and water seemed of more value to him than life itself, and he had to fight himself to maintain caution. He could get down into the notch without exposing himself to view from below. There he stepped into the saddle and, all at once, put spurs to his horse and sent it down the *bajada*, cutting for the east.

The pinned gunmen rose to the challenge and the air about him sang with lead. Bent low, he kept riding, firing across his horse's neck, hoping to keep Canfield and Lacey enough off-balance to throw off their aim. Then he was out of pistol range again, and he swung his horse around to look. Both gunmen had climbed to their feet, but a swift shot from the Winchester drove them down. After that, Nick headed east as fast as the horse could travel.

He reached the willows of Timble Creek

in about an hour, flung down in the welcome coolness and carefully watered the horse. He was equally slow about slaking his own agonizing thirst, then, restored, he rolled and smoked a cigarette. The sun was by then about two hours above the horizon. It would be well past dark before Coyle could reconnoiter the situation and get his force reorganized. By then the first riders should begin to appear from Snake Slope.

Mounted again, Nick rode for a long while along the creek, reluctant to leave its pooled shadows. Presently he had to, and he headed on a slant toward the deadline edge of the basin. A little later he came upon Pace Erskine, who stared at Nick's sweat-salted clothes.

"Somebody try to barbeque you?" he asked.

"Amounted to that. Seen any sheepers?"

Pace shook his head. "Quiet so far. What did you do?"

"Scrambled Coyle's puzzle a little." Nick went on to explain, concluding, "I hope Quince got a bunch of men started our way real fast. Once Coyle figures out that I only pulled his whiskers, he'll get back to business. Seen the other boys?"

"I met Bronco an hour ago," Pace reported. "He said nothing's happened in his section, or Andy's, either. But we can't keep this up very long, and I've got a feeling we're figuring Coyle wrong, anyhow."

"What do you mean?" Nick asked.

"Coyle's smart enough to know he can't fight his way down the slope, then along the railroad to wherever he's going. It would cost him every sheep he owns. Those items he cares about—or what they're worth to him—if not his men."

"I know that. But he don't seem worried."

"He's got a powerful lever, Nick. What if he gives us a choice—safe passage for his sheep or he'll plunge the whole damned country into war, including the outfits who aren't in any danger from his sheep. He's got things set for that, and he could spread bloody hell as far as he wanted, the touchy way things are. Ever think of that?"

"Yes," Nick admitted. "But the slopers sent us up here, didn't they? I don't think they'll scare out."

Pace looked at him out of jaded, somewhat cynical eyes, then smiled. "How many outfits are represented here?"

"Five."

"All right, and there's a dozen on the slope. All we got from the rest was an endorsement, and that could be changed mighty fast. They paid a hard price in the other war for a peace that left nobody satisfied. I'd bet if Coyle offered a halfway reasonable compromise, they'd think twice before they turned it down."

Nick said explosively, "He wouldn't keep a bargain a day longer than it suited him."

"Just the same," Pace retorted, "if he made

the offer and the cowmen turned it down, they'd get the blame if another war broke out. They're willing to threaten Coyle, but if they find out he can't be bluffed they'll start figuring things over again."

"I hope you're wrong, Pace."

"So do I."

A mounting anger goaded Nick as he rode on through the day's dying heat. Deep in his mind all along there had been the question that Pace had put into words. Only the outfits immediately threatened by the oncoming sheep had been sufficiently aroused to put men up here. At that time it had not been realized how cunningly Coyle would operate to swing the sheep country in behind him. Now, instead of a limited, local fight, there was a prospect of widespread trouble into which the whole slope would be drawn inevitably, with all the costs and horrors of the first war to be undergone again, with everything in the balance and a horde of sheepmen all too ready to take over the entire country.

By the time he came upon Bill Jarvis in the midsection of the deadline, Nick was in a state of private rebellion. He was fighting the temptation to communicate his feelings to Bronco, to join with him and Andy and take steps to make sure Coyle never wangled the kind of weak-kneed compromise Pace had suggested. It was a hard urge to put down.

"Dull as a church party around here," Bronco reported. "You responsible?"

"Might be. Right now Coyle's trying to figure out why I threw a few shots into his camp."

"*You* did that?" Bronco said, astonished.

"I know. I gave you boys hell for much the same thing, but this time it had to be done or by now there'd be sheep in the basin."

"How long will it hold 'em?"

"Not long, I'm afraid."

Leaving word that he would be out presently with food, Nick headed for camp. The intensity had gone out of the heat and the evening breeze was stirring. As he topped the last rise and could see down to the camp, he experienced a sudden excitement. A number of horses stood about down there. Possibly they were Coyle's, but Nick had a feeling it was the first party to show up from the slope.

He rode on cautiously until he was sure the latter was the case. The horses, nearly a dozen, wore familiar brands, Tin Cup and his own ranch iron, the shoe sole outline called Moccasin. Somebody let out a whoop when Nick was recognized.

Pat Tracer, who owned Moccasin and was Nick's boss, had a look of temper on his sharp, weathered features. "Quince explained what that damned sheeper's trying to do up here," he said, when greetings were over. "And you boys have done a good job. There's more men on the way, all you can use. What do you figure this bunch ought to do first?"

"Scatter 'em along the deadline, will you?" Nick answered. "And send my boys in. They're hungry and need sleep. And there's something you'd better think over, Pat. Coyle's apt to offer a deal."

"What kind of deal?"

"Safe conduct through our country or war bloodier than ever before. He's got the makings in the palm of his hand."

With a growl, Pat said, "You know I wasn't one who wanted to quit the first time, Nick. And this trip it's got to be a finish fight or we'll have tramps all over us every summer."

"But how about the other outfits?" Nick insisted. "The ones who did want to quit before and haven't put men up here this time? What'll they say once they learn Coyle's got the whole sheep country ready to back him?"

"Depends," Pat reflected, "on which way Coyle means to go from here. The outfits he'd run over would probably fight it out, regardless. The ones he'd miss, or promise to, might be more peaceably inclined. I dunno, Nick. And nobody will till the showdown."

For all his worry, it was a relief to Nick to have men enough to guard the deadline properly. Laramie, the Moccasin cook, was in Pat's party and had taken charge of the considerable job of feeding so many men with the supplies brought up by pack horse. Nick was glad to turn the job over to him and, with his responsibility lessened, began to feel the weight of his fatigue. Shortly after dark, with new men out on the deadline in force, he turned in.

6

The camp the next morning reminded Nick of the other war. He awakened to find that a second and larger party had come in, representing Two Bar, Gooseneck and Wing I, so that all the ranches immediately threatened by Coyle were present. Most of the men looked hard-eyed, resolute. Bedding lay about the yard, with an assortment of firearms, ammunition and saddle gear. Bewhiskered, sun-scorched men grumped about, waiting for Laramie to sound the call to breakfast. Out by the corral Pat was in earnest conversation with Ray Morton, who owned Tin Cup and looked uneasy. Nick suspected that the fiery little Pat was already at work stiffening the fighting will of the laggards. The day relief of new men was ready to ride out to the deadline and left presently. Berg of Two Bar, Simpson of Gooseneck, and Ivers of Wing I went along.

"Those three are more anxious to get on the fighting line than Ray Morton is," Pace said at Nick's elbow.

Nick said, "I noticed."

A Tin Cup puncher coming up from the creek with a towel on his arm stopped to throw a hard, intent stare to the southwest.

"Somebody coming," he called to the camp. "And it don't look like any of our boys."

Nobody paid much attention, but Nick took a few steps into the yard and turned to look out through the sun-heated morning. All at once he felt an electric shock climb his spine and spread into his shoulders. Wheeling, he walked in quick strides to the corral.

"Coyle's coming, Pat," he said to Tracer.

"Coming here?" Ray Morton gasped. "He's sure got gall!"

Turning back toward the yard, Nick called to the men, "Those riders coming in are Coyle and his two Bosco pardners—the Corta brothers. You boys stay out of what's apt to be a hot argument."

Within five minutes Tripp Coyle rode in, flanked by Pilar and Tomas Corta. All three tried to look relaxed and casual but Nick, waiting for them, could see the signs of tension. It was a reckless thing, their coming here, and the belligerence in the eyes so closely watching made that doubly plain to them.

Ignoring Nick completely, Coyle nodded stiffly at Tracer and Morton. He said, "I'm glad you showed up. The wild rannies you put up here have given us mean, uncalled-for trouble. I sure hope you owners have got more sense of responsibility."

"Responsibility!" Pat snorted. "Coyle, nobody but the Lilyville sheepers is fooled by the way you've stacked the deck. So don't waste wind.

You've rigged a situation where you figure you can put your sheep across our grass for free. So get whatever you came here to say off your chest."

Coyle looked at the Cortas and grinned. "Hear the man say 'our' grass? Where'd he get the notion it's theirs? If he's right, the land office maps we looked at a while back must be wrong. They say it's government grass."

"Let's have the threat, Coyle," Nick rapped.

"I ain't talking to no hired hand," Coyle said, looking again at Pat and Morton. "Especially one with a wild hair like Marquis. He's raised hell up here, and he'd make matters worse if he could. I like peace and quiet."

"The bloody trail you left behind you so far," Pat blazed, "don't testify to that!"

The sheepman eyed him blandly. "We never done a thing that wasn't in defense of our sheep. Some cowmen got highhanded about public land they claimed was theirs and couldn't make the claim good, that's all. But I've got a fortune tied up in them ewes and don't want to get them bottled up down the slope by more land-hog cowmen. Now, wait a minute. I've got friends in this country, and you know by now that they're damned good fighters. They've been hemmed in on the poorest range in the country by your cattle outfits. They figure it's time they got a fair shake, too, and they're ready to back my hand.

Thought I'd tell you that because I'd like to offer a bargain."

"What's your offer?" Pat rapped.

"You cowmen give me your word you won't bother me, and I'll stay high on the slope and give you no cause for grievance."

Nick couldn't help letting his jaw drop a little. It would be possible for Coyle to cross along the line dividing the sheep and cattle country and do neither interest much serious damage. It was a cunning bait if a man shut his eyes to the probable fact that it was attached to a hidden trap. He saw interest kindle in Ray Morton's worried eyes.

Almost eagerly, Morton said, "Are you saying you'll stay off our graze if we let you go through without fighting you?"

"I'll stay off any outfit," Coyle said shrewdly, "that gives me no trouble. That's all I've got to say. See the other owners and give me your answer by sundown." He swung his horse and, the Cortas following, rode off.

Pat's voice sounded hollow. "Well, Nick, you called the cards. All any outfit's got to do to protect its own grass is play ball with Coyle. That's powerful bait, and Ray, there, likes the looks of it already."

"His offer wasn't worth the breath it took," Nick said hotly to Morton. "Between here and the Black Rock Coyle went where he damned pleased. Those outfits weren't organized, but we are, and the only reason he made the offer was to divide us again."

Angrily, Morton said, "We can't fight sheepers forever! You heard what he said about the other sheepmen being ready to back him! He offered to go through on the dividing line. Why not consent to that and fight him if he breaks the agreement?"

"If we don't fight him now, we won't then and he knows it," Pat said tiredly. "I know what you're remembering, Ray. Dead steers and sometimes punchers, burned buildings and haystacks. I had 'em, too. Nick seen his herd wiped out and ranch taken over. But look what the peace we thought we made really did to us. There's probably more sheepers in this country right now than cowmen. Coyle's given them a rallying point—but we've got one too because, if we crawfish a second time, we're done for."

"All Coyle wants," Morton said desperately, "is to get through to the railroad!"

"This year, next year and every year thereafter," Nick said with rising temper. "And let me tell you something. When we were holding Pilar Corta, he dropped a hint that Coyle's promised them land. Where'll he get it? This gap stops him. But once he's through it and safely on this side, he can maneuver the way he did coming here from the Black Rock."

"We've got no right to start that old hellfire roaring through the country again!" Morton insisted. "Coyle wants his answer by sundown. We've got to have a meeting and see what the other outfits think."

"Count me out," Pat snorted. "Coyle knows my answer already!"

Morton roped a horse, saddled it and rode off. Nick knew he was going to see the other owners and felt a powerful impulse to follow the man. He started to move toward the corral, but Pat put a restraining hand on his arm, shaking his head.

"A man's got a right to decide for himself whether he lives or dies, Nick."

"Pat," Nick said urgently, "I knew there was a good chance the outfits that won't be affected by Coyle would refuse to help us fight him. But when it comes to this bunch—my God, if Morton gets them to knuckle down we might as well hand over the range."

"Even Ray said we'll have to fight if Coyle breaks his agreement."

"Which he will, when he's got us split and can take us on one at a time."

"Son, we're only two votes against a lot of 'em."

A sudden, compelling thought came alive in Nick's mind. Without another word to Pat, he continued to the corral and picked out a horse.

He rode straight for the sheep camp again, the sun hot on his shoulders and throwing the black shadow of himself and horse across the brassy earth. As he came over the last rise, he halted his horse for a moment and took a searching look at the camp. His hunch had been right. With the cowmen massed for a potential showdown, Coyle was out with the flocks and most of his men were with him. Nick could see only the old cook working with his skillet. A moment later he saw a skirted figure come down the steps from the sheep wagon.

He rode in.

Carlita Corta stared in hostile bewilderment as he approached. He was not surprised to see that the old Basque cook had picked up a rifle, which was trained on him squarely. A rising temper gleamed in the girl's dark eyes.

"You have the nerve to come here!" she breathed. "And I hope you have the sense to see that Augustine can kill you real quick!"

"Yes, ma'm," Nick said. "Also that he'd like to. Carlita, I came here because we've got to talk. I know that you Basques aren't born mean. You've come in for rough treatment, being foreigners as well as sheepers. And I don't think you Cortas want to help Coyle plunge this whole country into war just for personal gain or even revenge."

"You have the big right to talk!" Carlita blazed. "What have you ever lost, Nick Marquis?"

"A ranch," Nick retorted. "Didn't Pilar tell you? I've got the big right, *señorita*."

She seemed surprised, even incredulous. "Why did you come here?"

"Because of something Pilar let drop. About Corta helping you get land for what you lost. That isn't according to what Coyle offered the cowmen, this morning. He promised to go through the country along the divide between the cattle and sheep ranges if they'll leave him alone. He's lying to one side or the other, and I think to ours. He's promised you land, and how can he offer both?"

"What do you think I can do about it?"

"I think you pull a lot of weight with Señor Coyle."

"That I am his woman, maybe?"

"I wouldn't know."

Carlita made a hissing sound. Augustine's rifle tightened in his gnarled hands. The girl said something commanding in their tongue, and the cook subsided.

"So what would you have me do?" she asked finally.

"You Cortas are full of hate, but I don't think you're Coyle's kind. If you're his woman, there'd be a reason why you have to be, maybe to get his help. So it's like this. Help me prove his real intentions to the cowmen before they accept his offer, and I think I can guarantee you a place in this country and a chance to live like the kind of people I think you are."

"You think we would trust a cowman ever again?"

"Do you trust Coyle?" Nick asked.

"I do not trust him. But I can manage him."

"How?"

"Tripp Coyle is in love with me—though I am not his woman, yet. But as long as he thinks that some day I might be I can trust him not to betray my brothers and me."

"All you really want," Nick said patiently, "is to get set up again on a sheep ranch like you lost to some land grabber you call a cattle king. All right. This range has accepted the right kind of sheep outfit, the ones that pay taxes and support the country and do something for it. Not chiseling grass pirates like Coyle is."

"In this country," Carlita said with bitterness, "the treasure goes to the strong. That we have learn', Nick Marquis, and learn' well. And Tripp Coyle is strong."

"Then I was dead wrong," he mused. "With a Basque as with a Coyle, treasure comes before decency and honor."

The words stung. The eyes of Carlita Corta widened; he watched a deep intake of breath stir her breasts. A long-fingered hand made a slight protest, then fell limply at her side.

"You kill' my dog," she said softly, "yet in my heart I know I made you do it. Maybe for that I do not hate you now. But I could not do what you ask without my brothers' permission. And that I could not get. They have sworn revenge for the death of our father, for the shameful nakedness of my body that day. And now Pilar has sworn to cut out your tongue for what you hinted of me and Tripp Coyle. Yet you are so very wrong. It is not the treasure a Basque puts before honor. It is death before dishonor. Those are old words but they are true with us Cortas. You go now. It is very bad for you if they catch you here. That I think you learn' the other time."

Nick knew that he was not apt to see this gentler side of Carlita Corta again, and for a moment he looked into her beautiful eyes, trying to reach her will, to change it and her thinking. He knew it was no use. He swung his horse and rode out.

As he traveled through the day's piling heat, Nick's jaw set in grim and bitter lines. Instead of heading back to the Moccasin camp, he turned northwest along the deadline, meaning to find the ranchers Morton had gone to talk to and get a few things off his chest.

The first riders he came upon were Pat Tracer and Andy Baggett. Both men wore a look of repressed fury that projected across the distance to Nick.

"It's decided already?" Nick asked, amazed.

Pat nodded. "They're going to see Coyle. They'll agree to lay off of him as long as he stays on the divide. They'll threaten to fight the minute he strays. They call it a last-ditch effort to keep the peace, but I call it a mighty big victory for Tripp Coyle. Once he's through the gap, he'll laugh at their foolishness."

Softly Nick said, "Is Moccasin still holding out?"

"You know the answer already. And I just hired us four more men. Andy, Bronco Bill, Quince and Pace Erskine. When they heard what their outfits were going to do, they quit in nothing flat. Sorry, Nick. You won't have any more men than you had before."

"All I want to know is where we make our stand."

"Here at the gap. The one place where you've got a chance to hold Coyle back."

"But if he does break through?" Nick asked.

"Then we'll fight him every step to the railroad."

The four horsemen rode in slow, stubborn patience up the slope toward Chimney Rock. Nick sat his mount in the rock's wide shadow, noting their nervousness and sensing the ghostly fears returned from the past to haunt them as they moved toward the camp of Tripp Coyle. Berg, Simpson, Ives and Morton, robbed of cause and thus of courage, slid troubled eyes along the slope as in the old days of hostility. The war they sought to avoid, at least to postpone, completely colored their minds and thus their uneasy alertness made them see him waiting below the rock. The brand of his horse reassured them and, at Nick's casual gesture, they turned slightly from course and rode up to him.

Nick said nothing until they had entered the shade, where they kept saddle, their eyes unfriendly because they sensed his contempt for them.

"Hoped I could catch you here," Nick said. "I don't aim to see you men go to Coyle and hand him the slope if I can help it. That's what you're doing, no matter what you call it in your own minds. Did Ray tell the rest of you Pilar Corta thinks they're going to get land out of this—land taken from the cowmen by Coyle and given to them?"

From the surprised way the others looked at Morton, Nick knew that detail had been held back by the man in his determination to avoid another fight. A scowl slid darkly across Morton's face, he shifted in the saddle uneasily and stared down at the ground.

"Did he tell you," Nick resumed relentlessly, "that Coyle's got the Lilyville sheepers so bloodthirsty they might make their own cause for a new war, even if he doesn't give them one?"

Angrily, Morton blazed, "Look here, Nick! Your job's finished, and I don't see where you've got any business—"

"You're wrong there!" Nick returned. "I'm working for Pat Tracer again, nobody else, and I've got my orders. Which are to hold this gap, the same as I've done. I'm holding it."

"How can you without our backing?"

"You had some men quit. Your best guns. Pat hired them, and they're staying here. Go on, Ray. Crawl into Coyle's camp if you like and tell him you don't want trouble. It won't make any difference. He'll still have to fight his way through the gap."

"Determined to start a war, ain't you?"

"You damned fool!" Nick said harshly. "It's already started."

Herb Simpson was the scrappiest of the four. He began to look impressed. Ryder Ives had the expression of a man who had made up his mind, then found his decision slipping. Charlie Berg was chewing his lip, his eyes troubled. Morton's temper was dangerously out of hand. He had got the thing settled, and all at once he knew control was being wrested from him.

Regretfully, Simpson said, "Nick, I lean your way, always have. This is the strongest position we've got. But fighting here after he's offered to go through on the dividing line is clean out of bounds. I allow he ain't to be trusted. But since he's made the offer, we're over a barrel. We've got to wait till he breaks the bargain to throw lead at him now."

Bitterly, Nick said, "I'm not asking you for a man or a dollar. Just don't invite Coyle to move in on the slope, with a pack of land hungry sheepmen right behind him. He won't as long as he's uncertain as to what might happen. Don't agree or disagree. Just go home and leave it to me."

"But what can you do?"

"I've held that man here quite a while, and he's running short of grass. He's got to move somewhere, and the other sheepers won't stand for him bringing all those woolies onto their grass. But he'd do it to have his sheep. I know that about Coyle, and if the sheepmen can be made to see it they won't trust him to share the loot on our side of the plateau."

"That'd just encourage them," Morton objected, "to help Coyle blast his way through."

"Ray, Coyle doesn't dare to blast his way. He needs a hold that'll checkmate us. The threat of war, which has nearly worked for him already. His weakness is that those big flocks consume a lot of grass. Leave them to it long enough and he'll turn on the men he's trying to get to help him. If that happens, there's no more threat of a general war. That's what I've planned on. Pat wouldn't let me attend your meeting, Ray, or I'd have explained it there. He said you men have got a right to cut your throats if you want to but not his."

"By God," said Simpson, looking at the others, "there's sense in what Nick's saying. And I'd sure rather trust to that than to Coyle's sticking to a bargain."

"Just don't make the bargain," Nick rapped. "Don't send him any word at all."

"I'll go along with that," Simpson said promptly. "Ray, if you're riding on to see Coyle, it'll be without my company."

"Mine, too," Ives added, and Berg nodded.

"You're declaring war on him!" Morton all but shouted. "And if he takes you up on it, you'll be cursed from one end of the country to the other!"

"If Nick can make his ideas work, he'll be thanked," Simpson contradicted and swung his horse. Ives and Berg followed. Morton cast a yearning glance toward the sheep camp, flung Nick a look of pure hostility, then rode after them. His was a lone voice that he knew would impress Coyle not at all.

Nick's jaw was firm and hard as he watched them ride away. He had gained more than he had dared hope, yet he still had far less with which to meet the situation than he had counted on previously. After the flareups here, it would no longer do for his men to patrol the deadline, which would be to invite five separate murders.

Staring out across the blazing distance, his plan came gradually to mind. The thing to do was to abandon the line camp, as well as the deadline, when the extra men from below had gone home. Coyle would at first take that to mean that the cowmen were letting their silence give assent to his proffered bargain. He would start his move into the gap, and it would be into instant trouble. That would throw him off balance completely and make him the more desperate in his need for grass. He wouldn't have to fight invisible enemies very long before he would be forced to revise his entire plan.

Nick returned to where Pat waited with the new men he had put on his own payroll and told them what he had achieved. Pat agreed with the wisdom of their playing a rough but elusive game. Nick knew the country thoroughly, had already decided upon a hideout. Pat agreed to keep them supplied. The wiry little cowman was in the fight heart and soul, and Andy, Bronco, Quince and Pace showed the grim satisfaction of their kind at the prospect of violence.

They chose not to go down to the line camp until after dark. When they reached the soddy it was deserted. They fixed a meal and ate. The next morning, suspecting that the place was being watched by a Coyle spy, they gathered in the extra horses, packed their beds, and rode down the slope. Some five miles down the country they broke up, Pat going on toward Moccasin alone, the others turning south. They moved for several hours, gradually cutting back toward Boulder

Basin. By late afternoon they had set up a new camp in a cave that was within an easy ride of the Chimney Rock lookout. There was a spring and a long box canyon into which the extra horses could be turned. There was little chance of the camp's being discovered by a sheepman since it was somewhat north of the sheep ranges.

Nick awoke with the realization that the day might see the first real clash. Once convinced that the cowmen had abandoned the gap, Coyle would lose little time in moving his sheep onto fresh pasture. Their simple camp breakfast eaten, the other deadline riders looked at Nick, quietly, awaiting orders. He told them how they would work it, a man at a time standing watch at Chimney Rock, equipped with a mirror for signaling another man on the butte north of camp as soon as he sighted movement of sheep or riders toward the upper edge of Boulder Basin. Nick sent Bronco to the rock for the first trick, putting Andy on the close-by butte. The others saddled horses and picketed them to be ready to ride on a moment's notice.

The long hot morning passed with nothing to disturb it. The watch was changed at noon, Quince and Pace going out. Most of the drowsy afternoon had gone when Quince, on the nearby hill, flashed his mirror into the camp where Nick and Andy were cooking supper. The two blazing impacts of reflected sunlight meant that a scouting party from the sheep outfit was heading toward the basin.

"Not yet," Nick said when Bronco and Andy moved toward their horses. "Just be ready. I'm going to spy on those hombres."

Swinging to saddle, he rode in behind the butte, dismounted and climbed to the top, where Quince waited. "All I've had from Pace so far is he sees horsebackers coming," the older man reported. "No woolies yet."

"They're feeling things out," Nick answered. "Too, Coyle'd want to locate the first new water before he gives orders to his herders. I'm going to keep tabs on them."

He went on, making a careful ride of it as he cut in and out through the draws and low country. A little later he reached a point where he could see his own old camp, which he expected Coyle's men to investigate. They did, in half an hour, appearing from the west and riding in toward the corrals, moving cautiously, expecting that if there was a trap of any kind it would be set there for them. Nick counted five men in the party and, as they came nearer, he could identify Coyle, the Corta brothers, Lacey and Canfield. They closed in on the camp from all sides, alert, ready for quick trouble. At last they were in the yard by the sod house, and Nick saw Coyle and one of the Cortas shake hands.

The party went on to the northeast, indicating

as Nick had guessed that Coyle wanted to locate a new campsite in disputed territory, having been unable to acquaint himself with that country previously. Nick knew where the next water was, a rocky spring some eight miles distant, and did not follow them. He waited where he was, a point of sufficient elevation and cover to serve his purpose.

Just before sundown the sheep party came back, riding faster, and he knew that Coyle had found the situation reassuring, his conviction set that the cattlemen had surrendered that part of the country to him. When the riders had faded into the twilight distance he mounted and rode back to his own camp.

There was no chance after the sun set for flashed messages from Chimney Rock so Nick took his men out there. Night was closing in swiftly by then, blotting out the country roundabout. Up to the last light, Pace had seen nothing more coming, he said as he ate. Yet Nick knew that the next thing to appear from the direction would be sheep.

"Probably," he told the others, "Coyle will move one band down to the springs, first, instead of risking all four. If he gets through, he'll keep it there a day or two, then bring up the rest."

They would need no light to tell them if the sheep came on before morning—the blather would be warning enough. "Keep mounted and

83

shoot over them. If that does no good, shoot into them. There'll be armed riders, and don't give them the advantage of mixing it. Set 'em afoot if you can."

They scattered. Nick rode beside old Quince for some distance, dropped him off and went on alone.

Before the first stars came on, it was darker than he liked. The action came without much waiting. Nick heard Quince's gun and dug in the steel, heading back. When he reached the other's station, the old man was gone and the sounds of the fight had moved. Nick was halfway to Chimney Rock before he could pinpoint the rattle of gunfire with any degree of accuracy. Then he realized that Coyle had chosen the easiest and most central route through the gap, another indication of the confidence he felt.

Soon Nick could hear the plaintive bleating of the sheep mixing with the shooting. The direction of the sounds told him that Coyle had finally taken the fatal step, crossing the deadline with his sheep—an open act of aggression. Nick could see the teeming mass close to the ground and above it the crosshatch of red gunfire in the night.

Then he was in the midst of the melee. The sheep had come down the gentle slope on a wide front and were milling and churning up a dust that hid all but their noisy protest. Ahead of them a dozen riders were cutting in back and forth, firing into the turbulent night. The deadline riders had succeeded in bunching the sheep guards ahead of the band, and now whipped in like Indians, fired and wheeled away. Nick saw a horse go down, its rider scrambling to clear himself from the leather. Nick hardly realized exactly when his Winchester began to buck against his shoulder.

Then he was wheeling in and out of the fight with his men. He fired again and again as he passed the wild, shapeless flank of the dust-hidden sheep, sending more bullets screaming over them. Others were shooting across the flock now, and all at once the fear-maddened sheep went wild. Instead of exploding outward in the way of cattle they sought instinctively to bunch tighter, climbing and piling over each other. Mixed with the shooting was their bleating, the shouts of herders and the shrill, urgent barking of the sheep dogs. Coyle's encircled men were driven to charge outward then—Nick dropped the horse of a man driving straight at him. He swung his mount to the right, saw another target and drilled in the last shot his rifle held. There was no time to reload and, jamming the Winchester in the boot, he pulled his pistol. He drove down the side of the sheep band, emptying the six-gun and seeing foot herders desperately trying to control the witless sheep. He did not fire at the men.

A good half of Coyle's fighters were unhorsed, the rest had pulled back, disorganized and unable to determine in the fast, violent movement whether the whole of Snake Slope had joined in the battle. The deadline riders swooped in on the sheep, shooting, yelling. The rearward sheep began to move at last, turning back upon their course, bounding in an abandoned flight to the rear. The movement ran clear across the bunched flock, packed, half-smothered sheep all too willing to flee in the one open direction. In less than five minutes Coyle's whole band was in a mindless run toward its former feeding ground, herders, dogs and guards completely helpless.

Nick let out a wild yell and fifteen minutes later he and his men were back in the hills, pulled down and resting their winded, dust-choked horses. No one seemed hurt.

"Time they get that one straightened out," Andy breathed through a dust-scoured throat, "it'll be daylight."

Bronco said with satisfaction, "If they ever get it figured out. The way we busted into 'em they didn't know but what the whole cow country was boiling in."

"And the longer they keep wondering about that the better," Nick said.

They pressed on to hide themselves as completely as possible before there was light.

7

By first light Nick and Quince were back at Chimney Rock. As dawn dissolved the deep blackness in the east, he could see out across the scene of the fight. He could count the hulks of four dead horses and a few white, smaller bodies of sheep. Beyond, the country was silent, empty. For the time being Coyle had his hands full recovering and recruiting that flock.

Grumpily, Quince said, "Any chance of them trailing us to our camp?"

"Plenty," Nick said. "But not without warning, unless we get careless. As soon as he can count on their having us located, we'll move."

"I'd give a lot to hear what they're saying."

"Wouldn't be fit for your delicate ears, Quince."

Swinging onto his horse, Nick rode along the deadline that still ran inviolate across the gap. He made his way north for a time, swung west and rode into hostile territory. An hour later he was seated on a knob at a close and dangerous distance from one of Coyle's bands. The band was restless. Nick knew why. The country looked grassed off in the close, devastating way a sheep band could crop it. Coyle would be forced to seek new grass speedily.

Word of Coyle's setback at the gap was bound to reach the Lilyville sheepmen before the day was done. Nick felt that in all likelihood it would give them pause. They would begin to think of their own ranges and the fact that somebody would soon have to support Coyle's sheep.

Nick was on the point of stealing away when he saw two riders, instantly recognizable as Coyle and the runty Lacey, break over the crest just beyond the sheep. The two did not stop, as he expected them to, but continued north. Once past the band they turned northeast. Maybe Coyle was looking for additional grass in the near environs. Again, he could be seeking a different way to get onto the slope.

When the pair had disappeared beyond a distant clump of juniper, Nick found his horse and mounted. He rode on a line that would bring him in behind the sheeper and his gunman. He lost them briefly in a drop of the terrain, and was forced to follow sign. A little later he realized that Coyle and Lacey were across the deadline and in the north end of Boulder.

He came down through the rock formation at the basin's end, moved up toward the far divide. The men ahead were riding steadily, unswervingly, and when he topped a rise he caught sight of them, far down Snake Slope proper, riding at a fast trot. Again he waited, fearful of crowding his luck. He was fairly convinced that Coyle meant to feint at Chimney Rock again while slipping the other three bands of sheep along this route onto good grass.

Or—and all at once another possibility struck him—this course would take Coyle in about two hours' riding to the ranch of Ray Morton. Maybe he hoped he could get some kind of an agreement out of the frightened rancher to let the sheep cross the Tin Cup range.

Running the matter through his mind, Nick decided against following any farther. There was nothing he could do to keep Coyle from talking to Morton, and certainly there would be a limit to what Morton would do or say to avoid trouble. That he was a weak-livered, easily frightened man had been known on the slope since the first sheep war, but an act of betrayal would end his days there as speedily as Coyle could ruin him.

There was a way to estimate Coyle's destination, and that was the time it took him to return. Pulling up, Nick found shade, loosened the latigo of his saddle, and settled for a long wait. Rolling a cigarette, he found himself thinking of Carlita Corta and the faint suggestion, in the way she had looked and what she had said, that except for her obsessive hatred of all his kind she could have understood him. He himself felt it was a shame that she had been driven into an alliance with a man such as Coyle—under other influences she might have been a woman worthy of any man's devotion, a woman it would take a strong man to claim.

Some five hours had passed before he saw Coyle and Lacey returning. The time checked precisely with that required for them to reach Tin Cup, spend a while in talk, and return. A deep hunch confirmed his belief that this had happened, and his only uncertainty was how much the sheeper had managed to win or wring from Ray Morton.

He let the two pass him and again followed them at a cautious distance. Once through the gap they surprised him by turning south, parallel to the deadline but on their side of it. He followed long enough to realize that Coyle was heading for Lilyville. Whether or not he had gained anything at Tin Cup, he now wanted to see the local sheepmen.

Nick broke off his stalking then, deeply disturbed, and rode back to his own camp. Andy and Bronco Bill were there, the other two riders having taken over the watch. They had eaten, and there was food left over for Nick, who ate hungrily. Afterward, drinking his coffee and smoking a cigarette, he told the two what he surmised of Coyle's morning activities.

"You used to ride for Morton, Andy," he concluded. "How about it? Would he sell us out?"

"Not for money," Andy said. "But maybe to

save his own hide. I dunno. He took a bad scare in the last fight."

"There's one way to find out," Nick decided. "If Coyle's calling another Lilyville sheeper meeting, I've got to find out what it's about."

"I wouldn't lay two bits on your chances of going to Lilyville again and getting back," Bronco said.

"I've got to risk it, but I'll wait till it's late enough for Lily to've found out something. They've been holding their meetings in her saloon."

Nick moved into the shaded coolness of the cave and stretched out on his bedding. One by one he managed to put the concerns crowding his mind into temporary suspense, relaxing by stages until finally he drowsed off. When he awakened the tag end of the day had gone and he walked out to where Pace and Quince now sat by the concealed fire. They had kept food warm for him, and he ate his supper.

Pace said, breaking a long, thoughtful silence, "You don't have to risk going to that sheep town again, Nick. It's ten to one Coyle knows by now that we're all that stands between him and slope grass, with Pat Tracer the only cowman really backing us. That much Morton must've told him. So he's in Lilyville to put his train back on the track with the sheepers after what we did to him last night."

"Could be," Nick agreed. "He might give them the choice of helping take grass from us or giving it to him themselves. But I've got to see Lily. The less guessing we do, the better." He talked on for a while. He did not expect another try on Coyle's part right off, yet the sheep-trader was a shrewd man and might fool them. The watch would have to be maintained through the night. He would try to be back to camp, at least into the hills, before daylight.

He saddled a fresh horse and rode south, skulking through the buttes and rocky mesas. This brought him for the first time in several years to range that had once been his own. He had a feeling of nostalgia and increasing resentment as he crossed it, and found himself lifting his horse to a wild run toward Lily's town.

Thus it was that he nearly rode into a party of sheepmen heading toward that place in the same direction. Besides confirming his belief that Coyle had called another meeting of the local sheep interests, the near run-in restored him to sanity. He drew rein, just in time, kept his horse quiet, and waited long enough for the sheepmen to get well ahead of him. Afterward he changed direction enough to avoid another such near-contact. Somewhere around ten o'clock he was in the pines above the town.

The meeting, he surmised, was probably now under way—hence it might be reasonably safe for him to ride in. Later there would be drinking, with men outdoors, some leaving the town, increasing his chances of running into trouble. A few moments later he dismounted behind Lily's place. This time he left his horse outside the barn, ready for a quick departure and fast ride.

He moved along the side of the big building until he could get a quick look at the street. He saw over a dozen horses, at Lily's hitchrack and in front of the mercantile directly opposite. He could vaguely hear somebody talking indoors, but there was not the usual racket of the place. He slipped back to the rear, found the unlocked door that let into the kitchen and entered.

The room was dark. The voice was louder, still indistinct, but Nick thought it was Coyle's. The dimly-lit dining room came next and on its far side an arch opened into the hotel lobby, where there was lamplight. The bar, he knew, joined the lobby on the side. He moved on, prowling soundlessly, and stopped beside the arch, concealed, yet finally able to hear Tripp Coyle's angry voice.

"You men are either behind me or against me! Make up your minds right now!"

The lobby was deserted. Nick drew his gun, crossed to the saloon door.

Tripp Coyle had his back to the bar that ran across the far side. Some twenty men were seated at the tables, their chairs turned so they faced him. They could not see the doorway but all at once Coyle raised his eyes from his temperish study of the audience. They widened.

"Don't anybody turn around!" Nick rapped. "Or move at all!"

"How long have you been here?" Coyle grated.

Nick moved in a little farther so he could see the entire room. Lily was at the end of the bar. Her eyes were wide and she had lifted a hand to her cheek. He spotted Lacey and Canfield, seated. None of them had the courage to turn and look at him.

"Long enough," Nick said, "to know you paid a visit to Ray Morton today and scared him into telling you I'm all that stands between you and slope grass. And that these people have the choice of helping you break through or of feeding your sheep till you can yourself."

He knew that both guesses went true to the mark. Coyle's face tightened with exasperation; then he confirmed them verbally. "So what, Marquis?"

"So I figured to point out there's a third choice. Sending you on to Utah, the way we warned you to go. The folks here probably mistrust already that you'd get off their grass if they let you on. Or that you'll whack up the slope with them if you manage to get on that side."

"You're an outlaw!" Coyle roared. "And, by God, we'll hunt you down! Help to get you is all I've asked them for, and if they've got sense they'll throw in with me before you start to work on them!"

Nick said, "Listen, you others. This man isn't out to line anybody's pockets but his own. He'll use you and betray you if it suits his purpose. His sheep are getting lean. I don't reckon you sheepmen like to see that. But you don't have to feed them. All he's got to do is head east. That way lies empty country with plenty of grass. There's a railroad for him to ship his wool and lambs. It's on the way to Wyoming. Why's he so stubborn about crossing to the Short Line if he cares anything at all about his sheep? He's got a hidden axe to grind, and you're fools if you help him grind it."

Nick's eyes slid constantly around the room. He could guess what was on the faces of the sheepmen only by the black wrath on Coyle's. That was enough to indicate that momentarily Coyle's whole scheme hung in the balance. This speculation heartened him.

"Keep him off your grass," Nick resumed, "and we'll keep him off ours—"

A shot rang out and one of the hanging lamps disintegrated. Some Coyle faithful in the audience had managed to snake out a gun. Nick wheeled, lunging out of the lighted doorway into the dining room as another shot plunged the bar into darkness.

He could hear men milling and cursing in

confusion as he ran through the kitchen. He hustled out to his waiting horse and went up. Coyle and his gunmen, possibly a few sheepmen converts, would be hot on his heels now, but they hesitated just long enough before risking a rush out of the bar into the shadowy light of the dining room.

Nick drove in his spurs.

His caution in selecting a fresh, fast horse for this ride paid off now. The animal lined out, pounding across open country, making for the hills. He was aware of a vague merging of shadows in the lighted section of Lilyville behind him—the first gathering of pursuit. Presently he knew that a dozen men were after him, proving that Coyle had won the support of several sheepmen in the man hunt.

Then his luck, which had been good to this point, quit him completely. He felt his horse miss a stride, then both himself and the animal were going over. Nick landed hard, scraping his face and a shoulder on the hard earth, stunned. He managed to roll and partly raise himself. The horse struggled to its feet and he knew a badger hole had thrown it. He yelled, trying to stop the mount, but it galloped on.

He rolled again, managing to reach the temporary concealment of low sagebrush. He heard his pursuers pounding up and flattened himself against the ground.

It seemed to him that he waited hours before he heard the sheepmen leaving town. His shoulder felt lame by then. A little later the back door of the roadhouse opened. Lily herself stood framed for an instant in the distant light; then she closed the door and turned along the covered walk that led to her private quarters. He saw her unlock her door and step through, shutting it behind her. No lamp came alight in the room and he surmised she was undressing for bed.

He moved quietly and quickly across the yard, rapped on her door.

He called out softly, "Nick, Lily."

The door opened in the space of a breath, and she hurriedly drew him into the room and closed the door again.

"Raised yourself a little hell tonight, didn't you?" Lily whispered.

He nodded, grimacing, and told her what had happened to him.

"You scared the daylight out of me," she said. "I thought you were guessing, but you hit the target. You've got some of them thinking, at least, that there might be two sides to the question of whether or not they all ought to back Coyle. There are good men and bad among them—some will act on the mere promise of gain, but the others need something more. After Coyle left they talked more freely, since the ones backing him straight down the line went with him. They all know Coyle's sheep are going to be suffering before long. They're worried about his taking over their graze—and maybe not letting go. The thing's hung dead center just now and could go either way. If Coyle can prove some of the charges he's made, they'll all back him. If he can't, some will hold back."

"Thanks, Lily. Is it all right if I take a horse?"

"Help yourself. And, Nick, I hope you realize how determined Coyle is to wipe you out. Don't let him get near you."

"Don't mean to."

Lily gave him a hooded lantern and he slipped outside, made his way quickly to the stable and saddled a horse. When he rode out of town he headed west instead of taking the direct north road. It was by then only a little past midnight, he judged. He had several dark hours left in which to ride wide of danger and make the hideout camp.

He reached the cave just as dawn broke over the hills. The fact that he was riding a strange horse brought Andy and Bronco to their feet. As he came closer they saw his skinned face. "What the hell?" Bronco asked, and Nick told them of the night's events.

"From here on," he concluded, "we're renegades. Coyle's branded us such and he'll hunt us down as such, excusing himself to the law if he has to with the fact that we shot up his sheep.

You boys fetch the others in while I get some grub ready."

The two punchers left. They had started breakfast, which Nick took over. The food was ready by the time his four riders were back in camp. They wolfed the meal in the silence men of their trade preferred. Finally, smoking and weary, Nick gave them their new plan.

"It's going to be tough," he said, "and you've got a right to back out now if you want." Nobody did. "All right. Coyle's in a tighter squeeze than we are. He doesn't want to bring the other cowmen back into the fight any more than we want to bring in the other sheepers. In a matter of days now, he's got to get his sheep onto new grass, while all we've got to do is remain a threat to them if he tries again to head them into the gap."

Pace Erskine nodded thoughtfully. "As long as we're a fighting outfit, the gap's closed to him. We proved that the one time he tried to go through. But the next fight's liable to be tougher than the last—it could be we'll have men to stop, instead of just sheep."

"Correct," Nick agreed. "I'll get word to Pat because he might be packing in here any time with more grub and ammunition. We'll have to live on what we can carry on the saddle and slip in to Moccasin when we need anything. Through the days we'll separate and rendezvous at night when they can't hunt us. Never twice in the same place but never far from the gap. If he can't catch us, he can't fight us—and he can't leave his sheep too long. A week could make Coyle give it up and turn east."

"Wonder what he's got in mind that makes him so bullheaded?" Andy said.

"Land," Nick answered. "Pilar Corta let that slip, and I think it was a real slip. If it was only a matter of keeping his sheep healthy, Coyle would have turned toward Utah in the first place. Which makes the alternative easy to guess. There's bunchgrass on the slope and white sage farther down, both as fine for sheep as for steers. The sage is good forage only after the first frost. So if he had the lower slope he could winter a big band here, the same as on the Black Rock, and move two bands through to market each summer. Doubling his profits as well as setting himself up a fine permanent ranch halfway between California and Wyoming."

"Think he'd divvy up with the other sheepers?" Bronco asked.

"Only if he had to. But some of them won't believe that till they find out for themselves. Like the Cortas. They don't like Coyle much, but they hate us plenty."

They broke camp, dividing the rations and ammunition among them, making up blanket rolls to be carried behind the saddle and stuffing their saddle pockets. The spare horses would be too cumbersome, and Nick would return them to Moccasin when he went down to see Pat. They moved east, driving their little cavvy, and after several miles they separated with Nick's orders to meet him after dark that night at Willow Springs, on the north end of Boulder Basin.

On the edge of cattle country now, and feeling reasonably safe, Nick went on alone, moving the loose horses at a brisk trot toward Moccasin. It was a ride of several hours, and he reached the ranch around noon, just as Pat rode in from his range. Pat showed astonishment when he recognized Nick and saw the horses Nick had turned into the big pasture.

Nick made his report and got Pat's endorsement of his change of plan. "And, by God!" Pat concluded. "I'm going over to Tin Cup and mop the ground with Ray Morton!"

"Wouldn't do a speck of good, Pat," Nick said. "The man can't help it if he was born short of guts."

"The others ought to know he's turned snake in the grass."

"Then tell 'em. But I don't want them to come into it again unless the other sheepers do. A week ought to decide it."

Nick ate his dinner and slept through the afternoon in the bunkhouse. He ate the evening meal and immediately afterward headed out on the long ride to Willow Springs. He carried spare canteens for his riders, so there would not be too frequent a need to visit the waterholes, which might be watched. His lame shoulder felt better, and as the early stars emerged a refreshing coolness lay upon the slope.

He reached the lonely springs around midnight. Bronco Bill challenged him as he rode in, and Nick stopped for a moment.

"Any trouble?" he asked.

"No," Bronco said, "but we sure got out of that cave in the nick of time. Me and Andy seen a bunch of 'em and turned Piute. We watched 'em track us into that camp, and they moved in on it like they expected a fight. We had to laugh."

"You'd better not play Piute too often. Right now the hardest wallop we can deliver Coyle is keeping out of his sight. But not out of mind. Does he get too nervy, we'll hit behind him—at his flocks."

The night passed without incident. Just before daylight they ate a cold breakfast and separated for another day of invisible patrolling, having agreed to meet again that night at a rock formation well south called The Needles. Nick drifted his horse for a long while, gradually cutting in toward the deadline edge of the basin. Finally he swung down, ground-haltered the horse and crept cautiously to the low butte where once before he had looked down on the sheep camp.

It was by then around nine o'clock and the camp seemed deserted. That fact gave Nick cause for a dry smile. He did not envy Coyle his position, for he had not only to protect his hungry sheep. He had at the earliest possible moment to track down the men menacing them in a vast, wild country. Even the old cook seemed to have been put to work, and it was probable that Carlita was out with the flocks, relieving a herder. There were no horses in sight and no dogs.

A powerful temptation rose in him to ride in on the camp and raise what hell with it if he could. He raked the place with a careful inspection and grew convinced that it was deserted. Presently he showed himself on top the rise, and still there was no sign of life below him. Returning to his horse, he swung up and rode around the end of the butte.

He saw her then, crouched on the side of the sheep wagon that had been cut off from his view before—Carlita, and she held a rifle. There was a dog beside her that apparently had informed her of his presence, and she was keeping it quiet with a hand holding its jaws. Meanwhile she would from time to time take a careful look around the corner of the wagon toward the butte top where she had seen him. So Coyle had not left his camp unguarded, and from her stance she looked like she would do a good job of defending it. After a moment she released the dog's jaws, and it began to bark. All at once, silent again, it cut toward him.

A wild recklessness, a hunch about this Basque girl, rose as Nick watched the animal. His rope was in his hand by then, and as the dog streaked silently toward him, he waited coolly, his eyes never leaving it. At the last moment he made a quick, expert throw and catch. A flip of the rope, as the dog tried to jerk away from it, and the creature went end over end. It was stunned, and by the time it had recovered, Nick, dismounting swiftly, had pig-tied it. He recovered his rope and rode on in upon the astonished girl. She had trained the rifle on him and her eyes tightened in fury.

"He isn't hurt," Nick assured her. "Just cooled off a little."

"Why did you come here this time?"

"I was going to burn your camp but changed my mind when I saw you. Got to wondering if you'd hold me prisoner till you can turn me over to Coyle, knowing he'd kill me."

Slowly she lowered the rifle, butt to the ground. "You are so soft Coyle will need no help from me to kill you. My brother Pilar—you could have beat him like Tripp Coyle beat you, but you did not. You gave him the water, the tobacco. Go, Nick Marquis. I cannot help them kill you."

"Carlita," Nick said softly. "I knew you're the right kind of girl. Knew it so well I was willing to risk my life. In working with Coyle, you're doing something it's not really in your heart to do."

She looked at him long and intently. "Please do not say things like that to me. It is not fair."

"It's true, though. I'd give a lot if I'd met you under other circumstances. I hate it that before long I might have to kill one or both of your brothers."

"I cannot change them. I cannot be disloyal or betray them. Please go, before you make me prove this. That I do not want to do."

Ruthlessly, Nick said, "Your brothers know Coyle's sheep are beginning to suffer from the scarcity of grass. Will they be able to stand it long enough for them to get the revenge, the land they want? Will you? There's a bloodless solution, Carlita. That's for Coyle to go into the country between here and the railroad in Utah."

"He will not do it."

"Why not?"

"So you are hoping to get information from me? Go, Nick Marquis, before I change my mind."

Nick smiled, touched his hat and turned his horse.

When he topped the far rise, he stopped to look back. She had moved out to the dog and untied it, but was holding it again. Her eyes watched him until he had ridden out of sight.

8

For the next several days the riders from Snake Slope moved like phantoms through the hills. No day passed without one of them narrowly escaping a fatal encounter with Coyle's men. Coyle, however, seemed content for the moment to feel out his opposition, without making a concerted attempt at a break-through. Then, overnight, the weather turned unmercifully hot.

Nick rode through that day with a strangely mixed feeling of elation and dread. The sheep were overdue for shearing, while Coyle could not undertake that until he was near enough to a railroad to ship the wool. The grass was all but gone, the lambs were fast growing past a marketable age. Action must come, forced on the tramp sheepmen by these circumstances. Nick did not see how the man could stay there any longer without risk of waiting too long even to save himself, let alone gain his unannounced ends.

On the fourth day of the brutal heat that lay over the high country, still and stifling, Nick gained an appalling insight into Coyle's emergency measures. That day the draws and hills and open spaces came alive with riders. Nick, constantly on the move, had the numbed wonder if the pressure he had put on Coyle had backfired, with the local sheepmen joined in the hunt in force now, acting for the sake of the sheep or in the knowledge that it was the only way to save their own range from Coyle. Whatever their reason, they were helping to clear the gap.

So constantly was he kept on the move that day, he was considerably relieved that night to find all his men waiting for him at Kettle Wells. They had had the same experience.

"Country's crawling with sheepers," Quince reflected, "and they're sure on the warpath. Whatever Coyle done, he's made it rough for us. We can't hope to hold 'em back for long now."

"Going to be another night move," Andy added. "And maybe this is the night. Hadn't we ought to ride back down to the basin, Nick?"

Nick was already considering that. "If that's it, they're covering every draw. If they're moving the sheep tonight, they'll outride 'em so heavy we couldn't come within shooting range. I won't lead you into suicide. You wait here."

Pace Erskine bristled. "If you're going down there, so are we."

"You'll get your chance at all the fighting you want," Nick promised grimly.

The horse he had ridden that day showed its fatigue as it carried him again into the night.

He rode boldly into Lilyville two hours later, apprised beforehand that there would be no sheepmen about. The lobby of the hotel was deserted, and there wasn't even a light in the adjacent saloon. The whole place had a feeling of crisis, of lifeless waiting.

The first person he saw on the upper floor landing was Kitty. When she recognized him in the gloom, she stopped, her eyes going wide.

"You!" she gasped. "You've got your nerve to come here!" Her face was twisted in fury.

Someone else made hurried steps behind her. Another of the girls, apparently moved by her outcry, came down to her door, saw Nick, and she also turned stiff with hostility.

"What's wrong with you people?" Nick demanded.

"You should ask."

Before he could speak again, Lily Falcone emerged from the dining room below. She appraised the situation instantly and with quick authority said, "Take Kitty back to her room, Mabel. And stay with her."

Sullenly Mabel drew Kitty back away from the stairs. Nick watched Lily in puzzled thought as he came down. He saw an immense urgency in her eyes.

"I'm glad you came," she said. "If I'd known how to find you I'd have tried."

"What's happened, Lily?"

"You remember Frank Ralston—the sheepman Kitty was going to marry?"

An ugly apprehension kicked through Nick at the way she put it. "What do you mean—was?"

"That's what's eating Kitty. He's dead. Hanged. It happened last night."

Nick felt himself start to shake with anger. "Rigged," he spat.

"I'm the only one around here who seems to believe that. The Moccasin horse you lost the last time you came here—Coyle got hold of it. It was found dead near Frank's cabin. There were signs of a gunfight. Frank was swinging from a cottonwood."

"My God!" Nick breathed.

Lily said, "Every sheepman in the country has joined Coyle, ready for a finish fight. You'd better go now. Even my girls think you're responsible for what happened to Frank."

Nick nodded, stricken silent. The situation had a deadly clarity now. His failure had been in judging the lengths of which Coyle was capable. The chances were a thousand to one that even the Cortas did not know what had really happened.

"Thanks, Lily," he mumbled.

"It's scarcely a thing to thank me for."

"I mean for keeping a clear head."

He was soon in the saddle, riding back into the hills, still unable to grasp the appalling development completely. Gradually, as he traveled, he put it together. The killing would be the work of Canfield and Lacey. They would have had the savvy to make the setting at Ralston's cabin realistic, and taking a life would be nothing new to them.

Nick had seen Frank Ralston only once, briefly, but even so he sensed the outrage the local sheepmen would have felt and understood the emotion that had driven them into Coyle's design. He felt pity for them and for the cattlemen on the slope who would die before the thing could ever be proved for what it was.

He had to put such thoughts from his mind, for the urgencies now upon him were crowding and crushing. Coyle could not get far in one night's march, would not try, once his sheep were on improved grass, for he would want to feed them up immediately. Snake Slope had to be warned of the development at once.

He returned to Kettle Wells to find his men nervously waiting for him. He watched the fury that clouded their eyes while he told them what had happened. They were deadly quiet in their reaction, saying nothing, their movements taking on a leashed tension. Mounted, they started down the slope to Moccasin as fast as their jaded horses could carry them.

Dawn found them at the squat ranch buildings and rambling corrals. Pat paced the floor as he listened to the news. "War," he said at last heavily. "There was never any chance it could be anything but war. And now we've got to fight it where it'll hurt us the worst."

"Coyle isn't through the gap yet," Pace said.

"We can't hold it against thirty or forty sheepmen. While we were trying to, some of them would be down here burning our buildings and running off our stock. That devil's rolled us over a barrel finally, thanks to a lot of help from Ray Morton."

"Morton'll claim otherwise," Nick reflected. "That we brought it on by not taking up Coyle's offer. That's what scares me, Pat. There's so many hostiles now, the slopers are apt to figure the less trouble they make the easier they might get off."

Dryly, Pace said, "It's a hundred to one that as soon as he got through, Coyle would have pulled that, anyhow. He's got cards up his sleeve he hasn't shown anybody, yet."

Nick nodded. "No man would go through what he has just to get his sheep to one railroad when it would be easier to go to another. It's land he's after, and it's come to me that maybe he isn't trying to reach a railroad at all."

Pat gave him a brittle stare. "Say what you mean?"

"Look how he'd have been sitting if we'd let him go through on the dividing line between the sheep and cattle ranges without trouble. He could have stopped somewhere around Saddle

Mountain, about halfway through, and started to build himself a ranch. He'd have the sheep country back of him, us in front. Then, little by little, he'd spread out our way—over us and all the other cattle spreads below him. The other sheepers would move down on his flanks."

"But his wool and lambs," Bronco objected.

"Saddle Mountain isn't far from the old freight road to Kelton. He was only feinting toward the Short Line at American Falls. Those ewe bands aren't for sale in Wyoming. They're stockers for a mighty big ranch right here on the slope."

"The lengths he's going to," Pat said, "makes that at least one sensible explanation. And he's sure got it set up pretty for himself."

"We've still got a chance to turn the tables," Nick said. "Let him get to Saddle Mountain as long as he stays on the dividing line, which I think he will. By that time there's going to be even more wool on those sheep, and the weather'll be hotter yet. If he stops to shear, it'll prove I'm right. The other slopers will be forced to realize it's what he intended all along. With their help, we've got a chance to drive them out over the Kelton road. Coyle's got a weakness he may be too insensitive to realize. Those Basques think as much of their animals as they do of themselves. He's completely dependent on them for handling the sheep, and I think there's only so much suffering they'll let the critters stand."

Pat was doing a little private figuring. Presently he said, "They'd be at Saddle Mountain in about two weeks, with the real hot weather just setting in. We could hold 'em on three sides till they'd grassed the place off, which they would by the time they'd sheared. There'd be only one way to go to get more grass without fighting and uncertainty. Toward Kelton and away from us. Nick, if you're right about them Boscos, you've got it."

"I'm sure enough to gamble on it, Pat."

"That's putting a lot of faith in a foreigner," Bronco said. "And a sheepherder, besides. What do we do meanwhile?"

"For one thing," Andy answered, "get some chuck and then some sleep. We've been leading a fast life."

Nick found that after two or three hours of sleep he was wakeful and restless. When he came out of the bunkhouse, Pat was gone. Laramie, the cook, apparently had been sent off on an errand, also, for the cookshack was deserted. Nick got the binoculars Pat kept in his office, filled the empty loops of his shell-belt, and dropped a handful of .30-.30 cartridges into his pocket. He caught a fresh horse and saddled it, returned to the cookshack and got a handful of cold biscuits that he stuffed into a saddle pocket.

He rode southwest with only a couple of daylight hours left. He kept to a fast clip, and when night came on he was halfway back to the gap. Shortly afterward he turned south into the runs he knew as well or better than any other man in the country. By midnight he was on a mesa from which he could see down into the basin near Chimney Rock. He counted a half-dozen campfires. The sheep had come in, and that part of the basin was bristling with armed sheepmen.

He waited there, growing drugged with his tiredness. Around two o'clock there was activity below that told him the guard was changing. In another two hours dawn had blanched the eastern sky, and as light came on stronger he could use the field glasses. It seemed to him from the horses and men that most of the Lilyville country was on hand. A number of men were outriding the flocks, far enough away to stop trouble before it could be carried to the sheep. Others were at the scattered fires, fixing their breakfast. Coyle's sheep wagon hadn't been brought in yet.

Not long after daylight more sheep came over the far rise and moved in on the grass. Nick's surmise that Coyle would feed them up before undertaking the long drive along the slope was confirmed by this movement. Its leisurely thoroughness indicated also that Coyle did not intend to make the long drive to the railroad before he relieved his sheep of their heavy, sweltering fleece. He would shear far short of there.

Presently Nick tightened the cinch on his grazing horse, slipped the bit back into its mouth, and rode back to Moccasin.

Coyle held his flocks in Boulder Basin for several days, on grass that had not yet been touched by cattle this year, resting the animals for the next long drive. He moved them through the gap under guard of thirty men. But afterward he turned along the range divide, as he had agreed, out of no charity but because, Nick suspected, he wanted to get his sheep safely to where he meant to hold them before he asked for more trouble.

By the time he reached the high flats and mesas around Saddle Mountain, Nick saw that time was doing its work. Many of the Lilyville men, their wrath cooled and their worry lessened now that Coyle was on abundant grass and no longer a threat to them, were pulling out for home, where other work pressed. Yet a number stayed, and Nick knew that these persistent ones were Coyle's true allies.

Thus Coyle reached Saddle Mountain with twice the force he had had back beyond the gap. And there he halted, with wagons arriving the very same day over the Kelton road with undressed lumber. Even as the big rigs were unloaded, work began on extensive shearing pens, so large and so well built that they were undoubtedly meant for permanent structures. The sheepwagon and camp were set up in the trees by the springs. In another year, if Coyle was successful, there would be a house there and barns and sheds.

Moccasin was directly north of him now, down the slope, with Tin Cup, Gooseneck and Wing I within easy reach. For year-around support of so big a sheep band, Coyle would need all of that range. If land was to be seized for division among his faithful supporters as well, the ranches east and west were also important in Coyle's design. Every outfit on Snake Slope understood at last what threatened them. They met at Moccasin on the night Coyle reached Saddle Mountain and did there precisely what Nick had warned he would.

"You were right all along, Nick," Herb Simpson said. "And we can thank you for keeping us from inviting him to do it. I say you've earned the right to keep on running the show and doing it your own way. But there's one thing that bothers me—why ain't the sheriff been around with a warrant for you and the boys? If he shows up, you'll have to take to the timber."

Nick said, "Coyle wouldn't want a sheriff poking around up here. For one thing, there're men right in Coyle's band who know I lost that Moccasin horse to him and never saw it afterward."

"Where do you mean to draw the new deadline?" Ray Morton asked.

Nick gave him a brittle stare. Morton was a

thoroughly frightened man still, having betrayed his neighbors only to find himself completely dependent on their help.

"I've half a mind to leave your range on his side," Nick said. "No man ever made a good deal with the devil, and if you were the only one to take the consequences, I'd let you do it. But we'll draw it on a half-circle starting at Pilot Butte, swinging north to the Moccasin Rim, then back. That gives him enough grass for the time they'll need to shear and no more."

"Why wait for him to shear?" Morton said, suddenly fierce. "Why not send him south now?" He fell silent when the others simply laughed. His fear had materialized, he wanted to drive it away speedily, or wanted his neighbors to do it.

The ranch owners saddled and rode south, determined this time to make it clear to Coyle that they stood solidly together. They were aware of the risks, of the lust for revenge in the hearts of many a man in the sheep contingent, as well as the venal desire for more land in them all.

Before they took the trail down from Moccasin Rim, Nick halted the big party and pointed out the terrain in the moonlight. Briskly, he said, "Coyle's need to divide us is all the clearer now that we know his real intentions, and he must have looked over this country pretty carefully before he launched the thing. We've got three gaps to hold instead of one, even with the deadline drawn this close in. It'll take every man we can put up here to do the job."

"He'll strike behind us!" Morton said. "He'll burn buildings and hay and shoot stock, so we'll have to pull back to defend our property!"

"Only," Nick retorted, "if his Basque partners and herders will stand for the sheep going hungry long enough. I'd bet my life that they won't."

"I don't see anybody giving up for the sake of a damned sheep," Morton mumbled.

"No, Ray," Nick agreed. "I don't reckon you can see how that would be possible. But you don't happen to be a Basque."

"Be damned if I know just what he is," Pat mumbled.

They were at the bottom of the grade when the rifle shot rang out. "Scatter!" Nick barked. "But keep on! We're going in!"

The shot had been a warning, as he had guessed, revealing that all approaches to Coyle's new holding ground were being watched. A rider went streaking out to warn the camp, but the cattlemen rode on openly, showing no interest in the bands of sheep to the right and left. As they approached the springs, a dozen men appeared on a line before them, heavily armed.

"We want to talk to Coyle!" Nick called out. "And we're coming in!"

Coyle's big figure was soon apparent in the center of the line. He gave some kind of order, for the others fell back, still with plenty of distance between them and the sheep camp. Coyle held a rifle, and his legs were spread solidly as he waited, not answering Nick's call. His men roughly equaled the number of cattlemen, and he didn't look easy as the latter rode up to him.

"Well?" he demanded finally. His eyes moved until they found Pat Tracer.

Pat said, "Nick Marquis is still the boss and he does our talking. All I've got to say is that we're backing him straight down the line. Including some new faces for you, Coyle, men you hoped to keep out of it."

"All right, Marquis," Coyle said, turning his attention back to Nick. "You shot up my sheep and you strung up Frank Ralston. Just the same, I've kept on the dividing line. But I've got to shear. So I'm building pens to do it. The wool can be hauled to Kelton when the wagons go back and we can drive in our lambs. Then go on with the ewes. What have you got to object to in that?"

"Nothing," Nick answered. "If it was what you really intend to do. But it's what you will do, Coyle, that we want some say in. We're drawing a new deadline, from Pilot Butte to Moccasin Rim, then back to Saddle Mountain."

A man came hurrying from the strung-out sheepmen behind Coyle. It was Pilar Corta.

"What is this?" he said to Coyle.

"You heard, Pilar," Nick answered. "We're

giving you grass enough to shear because those critters are suffering, and for no other reason. After that, the only place they'll get more grass is on the Utah trail. I'd advise you to take it. That's all I've got to say except that you Basques probably don't know Coyle got hold of a Moccasin horse and killed it there where his gunhands hanged Frank Ralston."

"Is that true, Tripp Coyle?" Pilar asked. His rough voice was plain evidence that relations had become strained in the previous period in which the sheep had suffered.

"It's what he'd like to have some people believe," Coyle snorted.

"Why didn't you call in the sheriff about it?" Nick taunted.

"Because we kill our own snakes, Marquis," Coyle returned calmly. "And it's plain you're trying to turn my Basque friends against me. You won't succeed. For one reason, Pilar has promised himself to cut out your tongue. For another, they've already had a bellyful of high-handed cowmen."

"And," Nick added, "you've also promised them land on Snake Slope."

Coyle flung a quick, hot stare at Pilar, aware for the first time, apparently, that that information had leaked out. Corta met his gaze in cold silence. The Basque was obviously concerned at finding the resistance had by no means been broken back there at the gap, as Coyle must have predicted. Instead, here was clear-cut evidence that it had actually stiffened considerably. Also, there seemed to be much that Pilar neither understood nor liked. Coyle saw the incipient danger in the man, and his expression changed.

"Are you forgetting your father, Pilar?" he said, his voice more moderate. "Jesus Corta, who burned to death tied to a wagon wheel?"

That did it. The poison in Pilar Corta spewed through him again. He flung a bitter, infuriated look at the cowmen, then turned and walked back to where the others waited and watched, ready to open fire at a command from Coyle.

The tramp sheepman stared at the ground, then looked up again. "If you've said your say, get out," he rapped.

"I haven't finished with you, Coyle," Nick said, just as roughly. "That deadline goes for men as well as sheep. The first one of either that crosses it is dead the minute he's seen. So if you're thinking of a little dirty work beyond the line, think again."

He knew that every other cattleman in the party felt the riffling of danger at his back as he did as they rode back toward the long, wheeling rim that made up much of the new deadline. But Coyle was not ready for a pitched battle, and the riders reached the grade, climbed to the rim top. Nick began to toll them off, giving them their posts. He divided them according to the difficulty of defending the three gaps they had to hold, and used up half the men available. Moccasin would be the base camp until the thing was settled, and the rest, Nick with them, rode in.

When Nick took a relief out to the rim grade the next morning just after daybreak, the sheep shearing had already started. Through binoculars, Nick studied the new layout, which had risen almost overnight. The Basques were doing the shearing, four or five of them working with snips, others moving the overheated ewes into the pens and out, a wool-stomper packing the tied fleece into the huge burlap sacks that the lumber wagons would haul back to the railroad.

The larger part of the sheep still ran loose in the half-circle afforded by Saddle, the rim, and the long range of which Pilot Butte was the prominent landmark. Nick saw plenty of men out among the bands, ready to fight off any kind of molestation. He rode on to the other two exits from this constriction, the gaps between Saddle and the rim and the rim and Pilot, where he changed the guard.

He felt that the gamble he had taken when he decided to yield the pass out of Boulder Basin was paying off. Instead of a deadline that had been some six miles long, this was short and impregnable except at the three exits, and he no longer had divided, uncertain men behind him. Too, he now knew the desperate measures of which Coyle was capable, and was set for anything. Once the man had the wool off his sheep he would act, and already he must be planning.

For a week nothing happened at Saddle Mountain but the steady progress of the shearing. That Tripp Coyle was crowding the work to the utmost was evident when at the end of that time there were more shorn sheep on the flat below Saddle than those with wool. Some of the wagons left loaded, then a big lamb band trailed out.

Pace Erskine, always a man inclined to the disillusioned view of things, made a comment to Nick one day when they were alone at Saddle Gap. "You're taking a load of worry off their minds. And it's still to be seen whether that wins the Boscos' respect or just heartens them to continue the fight."

"A hungry sheep's in more trouble than an unsheared one," Nick retorted. "And the grass down there already looks short."

"Sure, but there's plenty more our way, the same as to the south."

"All men aren't Coyles, Pace."

"I don't think so, myself. But it's easier to make Coyles out of most men than to make them into sterling characters."

With a tired smile, Nick said, "Pace, prying

into a man's life isn't one of my vices. But I've wondered sometimes what brought you out here to spend your life in a saddle. You've had schooling—you sure weren't brought up for this."

"No," Pace admitted. "Anything but. It just happened that I preferred a riding job—and I'm just naturally good with a gun. I don't mind telling you, Nick. I was trained for the ministry."

Nick couldn't help a look of shock. "You?"

"Me, but there were too many Coyles and Nortons on earth for me ever to love my fellow man."

"You make me think of Lily Falcone."

Pace laughed. "Thanks. Certainly not because of my beauty."

"Because something drove her into hiding, too, and turned her harder than she ought to be. You two ought to get together."

"We've been together a great deal."

"I never knew that."

With a shrug, Pace said, "It was a long time ago. Not here."

Quickly, Nick said, "Pace, I'm sorry I brought it up."

"I'm not. God knows who's going to live through the next few weeks and who won't make it. Lily and I—well, we were married once. She won't see me or let me do anything for her now, but I've felt better being around to see how it goes with her. If anything happens to me, I'd like you to know I put her up there, a bitter woman running a roadhouse. I ran out on Lily. She followed, and I thought it was because she wanted to take me back to a life I couldn't endure. By the time I discovered she just wanted to be with me, it was too late. I'd turned her against me and everything else she once believed. When she settled here, I came after her."

Nick said softly, "Keep trying for her, Pace. She could be worth it."

"That I know."

Three days later the last of the sheep were sheared, the last wagonload of wool departing for Kelton. It was like the chopping of a flag to Nick for the forage on the Saddle Mountain pasture was all but gone. But the sheared sheep were in good shape, strong again, able to trail indefinitely.

A day after the shearing was finished, sheepmen from around Lilyville began to return. Bronco Bill Jarvis made the first discovery of the increasing numbers around Saddle and reported it to Nick.

"Coyle don't need the Boscos," he concluded. "He's going to have help to spare. Look out for dirty work, Nick, and probably way back from the deadline, on our side."

The newcomers were armed and, from the number of packhorses, seemed prepared to stay in the field as long as necessary. Evidently the emotional impact of the hanging of Frank Ralston would last until relieved by an equivalent explosion of violence.

Nick knew that Coyle's strategy would be along the lines Bronco suggested. A strike or two at the isolated cattle ranches would force the owners to pull men off the deadline, weakening it to the point where Coyle would hope to break through. But he would not need to risk his sheep now. Instead he could concentrate on discouraging resistance on the slope, securing a hold on the new range he wanted and making it as permanent as he could.

Yet there was a way to turn his plans back on Coyle. A swift raid through the upper sheep country would take a lot of the recruits home in double time.

Grimly, Nick talked it over with the cattlemen. They agreed. Nick planned to send his old deadline riders into the higher country under Pace Erskine. As soon as they were well on the way, he would deliver an ultimatum to the local sheepmen.

Pace left with Bronco, Andy and Quince shortly after dark, traveling light and heading toward Boulder Basin. At dawn Nick was on the edge of the Moccasin rim, looking down across the big sheep layout. There was unusual activity there, giving him a strong feeling that something new was about to be launched. Nick rode on down the grade.

In view of the fact that most of the sheepmen held him responsible for the death of Ralston, it was a dangerous move, but he had to make it. He rode in toward the sheep, aware of the attention he had drawn as he broke over the rim to start down, of alerted riders and foot herders all watching him intently. He passed them in seeming indifference, heading straight for the enemy stronghold.

9

A great deal had been done to improve the camp at Saddle Springs. Tents had been set up in the shade of the trees. The arriving wagons had brought more than lumber and he saw a heap of new provisions. Men clustered about fires, cooking breakfast. But they were watching and listening.

Nick saw Carlita at the Cortas' fire, and was aware of the deep anxiety that crowded into her face at sight of him. Her brothers, too, watched him with fixed intentness. Coyle seemed surprised by the visit and more excited than concerned.

"You've sheared," Nick said to Coyle. "And you won't need all the men you brought back from Lilyville to help you trail. So I think they'd better get home."

"You sure get big notions."

Nick said, "Pass the word. I've sent a party of men into their home country. They're going to wait twenty-four hours for these people to get back there where they belong. After that, any ranch whose owner isn't there tending to his own business will be burned."

In the silence that followed, he could hear the blathering of the distant sheep. Men left the other fires and came striding forward, hostile and yet concerned.

Nick warned them as they came in: "There're a dozen men on the deadline waiting to see what happens here. If I don't ride back in half an hour, they're going to start on these sheep."

Coyle growled a warning to the others. Nick watched them coolly. They knew he wasn't bluffing about the men he had sent onto their own range. Coyle knew it and more—he was going to have much of his support swept from him again.

"All you've got to do," Nick said mildly, "is go home, boys. In time I hope to prove to you that Coyle, himself, had Ralston strung up to bring you in with him. Lily Falcone knows it and there are men in the camp who know it, too. Don't do something now you'll be sorry for in a few weeks. As for you Cortas, there's only one direction those sheep can get the grass they're going to need bad in a few days. South, in that empty country. Think it over before you try to break them out in any other way."

Carlita Corta sprang suddenly to her feet. Her eyes flashed at Coyle, and her body was taut. "I tell you, Tripp Coyle, it is not human to starve those sheep again!"

Coyle's gaze swung from Nick toward her. There was a surprised slackness in his heavy features for a moment, then his eyes brightened with anger. "So you are leaning the handsome *vaquero*'s way. Maybe you would like for him to tear the clothes off you and make you dance for him." Jealousy, raw and driving, crept into the man's rough voice.

Pilar's hand went to the handle of his belted knife as he stared at Coyle. Tomas narrowed his lids, his tall body pulling erect and tight. Seeing that, Carlita underwent a quick change in manner.

She said, "I have not forgotten that, Tripp Coyle, nor our father, nor the home we lost, the sheep, the land. But that does not justify some of the things we have heard about you—and I will not see the animals suffer again while we wait to make sure what is the truth. Nor will Pilar and Tomas. Last night we talk it over."

Consternation came into Coyle's face. "You own a thousand head out of twenty thousand," he said harshly. "To my mind that doesn't give you much say."

"We can take them and go our own way."

"Only," Coyle said, "if I let you cut them out."

"You forget that the herders are our friends."

Coyle laughed. "Their going on strike wouldn't hurt me much right now, Carlita."

Pilar Corta cut in then, saying curtly, "We will stay with our sheep. But you may be sorry you make it this way, Tripp Coyle." The Basque looked angrily at the others. "See what happens when you deal with a man who is not one of us. I almos' think it is true what Marquis say about

Frank Ralston. That it is Coyle who have him hung, not Marquis."

"Why, damn you—" Coyle began, but Pilar's brown fingers closed on the handle of his knife.

Nick knew that the time he had told his men on the rim to wait for his return had about expired. He swung his horse and rode north. He could hear the slam of his pulse in his eardrums, but nothing outward happened. He came to the foot of the grade and rode to the top.

Pat waited for him there and afterward, with binoculars, they kept watch on the camp. An argument was going on there now, men waving their hands and talking back and forth. Presently they saw horses being saddled. In the same way the Lilyville sheepmen had drifted in, they began to sift back toward home, though it was impossible to tell whether their break from Coyle was permanent. Coyle made no effort to stop them, which might suggest they had reached some new agreement with him.

Nick had set up a field camp on the Curlue, a small stream that ran down across Moccasin toward the Snake. There those not on the deadline ate and rested while remaining within easy reach should they be needed. Old Laramie had set up a canvas fly and did his cooking under it. Bike Johnson, another rider grown too old for regular details, wrangled the cavvy the ranchers had thrown together.

Riding in with Pat, Nick had his breakfast. After that he slept for a couple of hours, as much as he had rested in one stretch in a long while. He awakened tired and drawn in the heat that mounted steadily now that midsummer had come. He had a cup of coffee, saddled a fresh horse and rode back to Moccasin Rim.

Herb Simpson was there, with four of his punchers. The Gooseneck men all wore a look of tight-faced surprise. The moment Nick rode up to them, Simpson waved a hand toward the edge of the cliff.

"Take a look," he invited.

Swinging down, Nick walked over, Simpson beside him. Staring out toward Saddle, sun-drenched and simmering in the day's full heat, he was astonished to see that the big pasture was empty.

"They pulled south," Simpson said in a hushed voice. "Could it be you cut the ground from under the man?"

Nick's mind could scarcely credit what his eyes showed him. Not only had the bands vanished. The tents had been struck, the sheepwagon was gone. He shook his head.

"They're pulling back to better grass, all right," he said. "And maybe to get those sheep out of the way if bullets should start flying around here."

"Think they'll still try to drive us off the deadline?"

"I'm sure of it," Nick said, "or hit us in the rear. There's no way Coyle could cut his sheep around us without our knowing in time to set up a new front against him."

The hope Simpson had drawn from the chance that Coyle had given up left his weathered features, to be replaced by the old worry. "Where do we make a stand—here, or on our ranches?"

"Both."

"That'll spread us mighty thin."

"Which is why he wanted to get us guessing."

Nick rode on to Saddle and Pilot gaps, telling the men there what he expected. Later, at the Curlue camp, he picked up Ryder Ives and headed south toward the climb onto Pilot Butte ridge, which ran low and long up the east side of the big Saddle pasture.

They sighted the south-pointed flocks about two miles above Saddle, moving toward the pass to the Utah side of the plateau. But the sheep were grazing leisurely, feeding as they traveled. Only the sheepwagon and horse band had pulled on ahead. Cutting through the ridge timber with Ives, Nick went on.

Coyle had set up his new headquarters at an old abandoned stage station some five miles farther on. Nick studied it carefully through binoculars. The small stone buildings of the deserted station sat in a saucer by a spring. Once this had been a meal station on the Boise-Kelton stage line, and the feeling was strong in Nick that the tramp sheepman had made this concession to the Cortas only to placate them in their concern for the sheep. It was a retreat that must have been galling to Coyle, yet it solved his grass problem for a time.

Equally, it complicated Nick's. Coyle's force had that day been shaken down to men he knew to be loyal to him in whatever undertaking, not even excepting the Corta brothers. The Basques had by no means forgotten their hatred of a cattleman. With their sheep properly cared for, they would be of a mind to resume the initial intention in this vast undertaking. There wasn't much question that Carlita would go along with them.

"We'll have to wait and watch what goes on," Nick told Ives. "And we'd better locate a place with more cover."

They rode back down into the timber, gradually working to a shaded vantage point. There they loosened their latigoes and tied their horses. By the sun it was around two in the afternoon. Nick could see smoke rising from the chimney of the old stage building, where a meal was probably being prepared. Keeping a steady watch, he counted six men moving about and once he saw a girl's skirted figure. Some time later the men walked together toward the sagging old corral that held their horses.

"Now it comes," Ives said, in his excitement keeping his voice down in spite of the distance. "Which way'll they go?"

"That's what we came here to find out."

With the help of the field glasses, Nick identified Coyle, Lacey, Canfield and three Lilyville sheepmen who had thrown in with the tramp sheepman lock, stock and barrel. The Cortas evidently were not taking part in this ride. Coyle and his men caught out horses, saddled, then headed north.

"Going back down to Saddle," Ives commented. "Or maybe just to check on the sheep."

"We'll find out."

Mounted, Nick and Ives turned back north along the ridges, coming down to the edge of the timber, yet staying in cover. Nick was not surprised when Coyle went on past his sheep.

"Get back to camp," Nick told Ives then. "And spread the word. I'm going to keep dogging them."

"If they catch you, they'll hang you sure."

"They'll have a fight first."

Ives went on, swinging higher into the trees, then cutting forward. Nick kept on at the lower level. Below the sheep bands, to his surprise, Coyle and his riders turned west. For a moment he wondered if they were heading for the country around Lilyville, determined to drive Pace and his bunch out of there in an effort to bring the

135

local sheepmen back into the struggle. Yet Coyle did not seem provisioned for so long a ride.

Presently Coyle and his riders cut across open country and Nick swung back, studying another possibility, that Coyle might be trying to flank the riders guarding Saddle Gap, either for a direct assault, or to make his way on down the slope for a raid on some cattle ranch.

Nick reached the Curlue camp only a little behind Ryder Ives. "Coyle's got some more men stashed out somewhere," he said. "I've got a hunch, they're joining up for something. The most logical thing's a sweep down the slope in hope of making us pull out and go home to protect our buildings and ranch stock."

"We don't have much choice but to figure that," a man said.

"Maybe that's the way Coyle's thinking," Nick answered. "He's smart enough to know we're keeping watch on him, but he ought to be bright enough to figure something else. So far we've laid off his sheep, but if he strikes at our livestock or buildings, that's over."

"On top of that," old Laramie put in, "he's cleared his sheep out of the Saddle pasture when there's still a little grass left. Nick's right. If you're smart you won't fall for his trick."

The others were inclined to agree. It would be impossible to defend both the deadline and their ranches properly; it had to be one or the other, and the choice could only be made through shrewd guesswork. Nick divided the men in camp equally and sent them out to reinforce the men at the gaps.

The sun was setting by the time they were all in place, having been careful not to advertise what they were doing. The slope breeze came up as it usually did with the first long shadows, and its cooling breath was welcome to the men hidden among the hot rocks. Night came on and the stars emerged.

The trouble erupted at Pilot Gap. With the first sounds of gunfire the four men at Saddle Gap and the five on Moccasin Rim hit leather. By the time they plunged onto the slope lifting to Pilot Gap, discarding cover for speed, the firing had become brisk and, a little ahead of his party, Nick could see the streaking fire flashes that cut back and forth.

The sheepmen had dismounted, horseholders taking their animals off to one side. Pounding in, Nick's men opened heavy, steady fire. The chips were down now, neither side having any further reason for restraint. The fate of Snake Slope hung in the balance in this violent, starlit hour.

The open charge was Coyle's first intimation that his attempt at deception had failed. That it should be from their rear from comparatively open country, seemed to surprise the sheepmen. All at once they were thrown onto the defensive, forced to protect themselves on two sides. Yet they rallied to it quickly. In a moment Nick was forced to wheel back.

Shouting an order to dismount, Nick hit the ground. He sent his men in on a half-circle, hoping to hem Coyle in. The rock that lay along the base of the ridge made good cover but was blinding so that presently the strung-out cattlemen were out of touch.

They fought individually by instinct. Nick had brought his rifle from the saddle boot, and started to climb up the slope, making quick runs from rock to rock. When a bullet shrilled deadly close to him, he knew he had been seen. He was caught in mid-run and went flat. A second bullet ploughed into the soil ahead of him. He saw the flash of a gun and fired. He heard a man's short, involuntary cry.

He crawled on to the closest cover. Neither he nor his men dared to move in too near for fear of getting into the fire from the gap. They settled then to the grim purpose of making it costly, if not impossible, for the sheepmen to pull out.

10

Serene above this violence ran the early night sky, aloof from it were the echoing rocks. The cattlemen on the gap, enheartened by a quick recovery from their initial peril, poured in a fire from enough elevation to score. Twice, three times, a man called out in pain or cursing.

It was soon evident that the sheepmen were concentrating on pulling out. Probably they had hoped to take the gap and hold it, or borrow the cowmen's tactics of hitting hard and vanishing into the night. Now neither plan was working. They began to weave their fire through the rocks about them, their fighting sharpened by desperation. A glancing bullet took Nick's hat from his head. Recovering it, he began to slide backward, not daring to let one of Coyle's men get in behind him, still unable to see a target.

He held his fire temptingly, and all at once men came scrambling his way, on their hands and knees, trying only to get outside the ring of hostility that had been clamped about them. Nick picked his man and fired and after that they were all pouring lead his way. When the flurry was over, they were gone, all but one still shape.

Knowing the sheep party was breaking out of it, Nick shoved erect. He saw other men up and racing toward the horses, any mount they could get hold of. Others were fighting a rear-guard action. In a moment they were gone. The men on the slope dusted the heels of the horses as they pounded off into the night.

Searching through the rocks, the cattlemen found three dead sheepmen.

"Wouldn't you know it?" Herb Simpson said harshly. "Coyle and his gunhawks came off easy, while their tools took the jolt."

"They know how to take care of themselves," another man answered.

"Yeah," said Simpson. "If they were even in on it."

Several of the cattlemen could report close calls but none had been hurt. Elevation had helped those in the gap, while Nick's party had been able to remain more or less stationary among the rocks while the sheepmen were breaking out.

They dispersed to their previous stations. There was little chance that Coyle would muster another attack tonight. With Pat and Herb Simpson, Nick rode back to the camp on the Curlue.

The place was deserted. Pat said in puzzlement, "I wonder if old Laramie and Bike pitched into it? Don't remember seeing them afterwards."

"If so, they'll be back," Nick said. He walked to the creek and looked across to where the horse band had been kept. He could find no sign of the animals. Worried suddenly, he returned to camp and swung onto his own horse.

He rode a wide circle on the far side of the Curlue but could see no horses nor any sign of the old wrangler.

Returning to camp, he reported to Pat.

"Think Coyle's gone in for horse stealing?" Pat said. "Or was he trying to set us afoot while he raids the lower country?"

All at once Nick had an ominous feeling that there was more to the night's venture than had been apparent so far. He sent riders to the other stations, but neither Bike nor Laramie had been spotted by any of the cowmen, nor had they been seen at the fight.

Nick slept uneasily that night—then, at daybreak, Bike Johnson rode in. He came from the rim, looked unharmed, but his seamy old face was set in shock.

"They got Laramie," he said in an exhausted voice, staring with dull eyes at Nick. "And they're going to hang him like they say you hung Ralston if everybody ain't off this deadline and on his way home by noon."

Nick could only stare hard at the oldster.

"Three of them sheepers come into camp right after the shooting started last night," Bike resumed. "At first we thought it was some of our boys after more shells or something. But it was Coyle and them two gunswifts of his. They had us covered before we realized what was up."

Nick swore silently. He blamed himself for the

oversight of leaving the camp unguarded. After Ralston's lynching, he might have expected something like this.

"That Coyle means business," Bike said urgently. "They're pretty riled about losing men last night. They'll sure kill old Laramie if we ain't off this deadline when the time's up."

"That I believe," Nick said heavily.

Bike Johnson went on to opine that there was no chance of freeing Laramie. He had been taken to the old stone stage station, an impregnable place in itself, and a dozen men were there to guard him. Bike had been taken along to carry the threat to the cattlemen and Nick had to admit the old man made his story convincing.

Others were hurrying in now, Bike's sudden appearance from the direction of the sheep camp having aroused curiosity. As they heard what had happened, they all went grimly silent, the triumph in the night suddenly robbed of its satisfaction.

"If we give up this deadline," Ray Morton said furiously, "there ain't another place to stand between Coyle and our home ranches!"

"You'd give up Laramie?" Pat asked.

Morton appeared ready to do that until he saw the look on the other men's faces as they stared at him, some in sheer disbelief, others in sudden hatred.

"Now," said Simpson, "he's ready to fight to the last man's life, so long as it's another man's life. Why don't you go up there, Ray, and offer to swap yourself for Laramie? You're a ranch owner, while Laramie's nothing but a broken-down cowboy, just good enough to cook."

Ryder Ives said, "Coyle wouldn't swap. He knows we'd probably give a sick steer for the damned coward."

Wheeling angrily to Nick, Morton said, "Even if we give up the deadline, Coyle won't turn Laramie loose! He'll hold onto him till he's got everything he wants from us!"

"Maybe so," Nick agreed. "But we won't let them hang him at noon. Break camp, boys, collect your men and go home."

Coyle and his gunmen had scattered the cavvy, but had not bothered to drive them far. Some of the men found the horses and hazed them back. It was a grim, discouraged group that broke up two hours later and rode off in separate directions.

Along with Nick and Bike, Pat said, "Morton's right in that this won't get us Laramie back as long as Coyle can make use of him. But you're right, Nick, in that it's the only thing we can do."

Nick said, "They won't be able to keep that big a guard on Laramie all the time, boys. Especially if they move the sheep our way from Saddle Mountain."

"You mean you're going to try for him?" Pat asked.

"What else?"

He rode with the others toward Moccasin for three or four miles, then swung west. He made a wide circle, and it was just at noon when he slipped back to the hills north of Saddle Gap.

It was some hours later that his search of the plateau below with field glasses was rewarded. Tripp Coyle rode into view, leading eight men. They approached Pilot Gap warily.

Nick could see the excitement that energized them when they realized that no resistance materialized even when they rode through the pass.

Three or four men came back down to bury the dead left there by the short, hot gunfight in the night. The others rode on to inspect the grade climbing up to Moccasin Rim, then came on to Saddle Gap. Nick's position was too far up for them to stumble onto him, and he lay quietly until they had ridden south again.

In another two hours the sheep were coming back, Coyle losing no time in consolidating the gains he had made. Riders climbed to the top of the Moccasin grade and fanned out up there, then the first ewes came up.

Coyle was feeling his way gingerly, and Nick viewed every step. The sheep were held on the mesa above the rim, while Coyle's riders moved on.

Several miles north of Saddle, lower on the

slope, ran a ridge that was the natural dividing line between the winter range and that used at more clement seasons of the year. Below it, where the land flattened, white sage was the main growth. Above the ridge grew bunchgrass, also excellent forage. Curing on the stalk in the hot dry air, it was natural hay, and it bore a heavy seed crop that was rich as grain. The adjacency of these two excellent yearly crops throughout this part of Idaho and Nevada and down through the Owyhee desert of Oregon gave cattlemen an opportunity rare on the western ranges, enabling them to run their steers in the high country or in the more sheltered lowlands according to the season, with rich natural feed in both areas.

This dividing ridge became an extremely valuable asset to Tripp Coyle, who probably could never have fought his way to it had he not chosen the means he had used. It ran for some fifteen miles, and there were only a few places where it broke enough to permit the easy passage of men or animals up and down. On the same day he moved out of Saddle pasture, Coyle set up guards at each break. From those eminences they could watch the lower country day and night. Guards could also patrol the length of the ridge. At the first sign of suspicious movement below, smoke signals would quickly carry a warning across the whole slope above.

Coyle's move had trapped a number of cattle

above the ridge, and Coyle's first move was to run them out. As the steers and loose horses poured down through the break onto the winter feed, Nick eased back from his vantage point. Shaking with anger, he found his horse, mounted and rode off to scout Coyle's camp at the old stage station.

The place was heavily guarded, and there seemed no prospect of freeing Laramie immediately.

Within three days the tramp-turned-landgrabber was entrenched in his new position. On the following night Lily Falcone appeared at Moccasin. Nick had been aroused at the sound of the horse coming in and was standing half dressed in the doorway when she arrived. Her horse was winded, her hair streamed loosely, and he knew she had ridden long and hard.

"Lily!" he gasped. "What brings you here?"

He helped her down, and she sagged against him. "They burned me out," she said in a choked voice. "Pace got in touch with me. The sheepmen set a trap for him and his boys. They planned it in my saloon. I tipped Pace off—and they knew I had to be the one who did it. They said they'd give me a dose of my own medicine, since Pace was there to burn them out."

"Are the boys all right?" Nick asked.

"So far, but in trouble. The sheepmen are after them hot and heavy. They've heard that Coyle won out down here. They're anxious to get in on the spoils."

The woman was obviously so spent that talking was difficult. Pat had awakened by then, dressed and come out. They took Lily into the house and Pat started a fire to heat some coffee.

It had been Nick's suggestion that Pace get in touch with Lily. Whatever the personal bitterness between them, he knew, she would be of service to the slope riders if she could.

"I put my girls in the hack and sent them down to the railroad at Wells," she said. "That part's all right because I never want to go back to that business again, anyhow. But the sheepmen are on an organized search for your men now. Pace can't hit back because any place might become a trap. I had to tell you. If the slope's lost, they're not doing any good up there, and you ought to call them in."

"The slope's not lost," Nick said savagely. "And they're doing good as long as they keep the divide sheepers in that country. I'm going to try to break out Laramie—then try to get in touch with Pace. You've got to stay here, Lily."

She shook her head. "I'll go on to the Short Line and catch a train out. There's no reason for me to stay in this country any longer."

"There's plenty of reason, Lily. And you know it."

The sharp look she gave him made him

understand that Pace had not told her he had communicated their secret.

"So?" she said.

"A woman can't run away from it any more than a man can, Lily. You ought to know that by now."

"He—he told you?"

"Yes. Stay here on Moccasin until this fight is over. All of it—Lily Erskine."

He had never expected that he would see this woman crying. Now, suddenly, he did.

11

When dawn came over the Rockies once more to set fire to the great desert, Nick was in a nest of lava rock west of the stage station. Under cover of darkness he had passed between two of Coyle's outriders, using a difficult climb known only to men with experience in that vicinity.

For a long time nothing stirred below. Finally vague sounds of awakening men and horses reached him through the growing light. Once or twice he thought he saw a dim shadow pass between the station house and corral, and had the uneasy feeling that he had been discovered, that the men below him had been alerted. Then it was light.

From the lava outcropping his spyglasses showed him the smoke of a morning fire drifting up from the station's chimney. There were five or six horses in the corral and a man was posted on a knoll behind the station to keep watch on the surrounding country.

As he used his glasses, Nick was carefully and systematically playing the reflection of his shaving mirror in brief flashes about the camp. After fifteen minutes of patient waiting, he saw the distant sentry hurry down from the little hill and disappear among the buildings. In a short time he reappeared and resumed his station. Presently he saw a man saddle a horse and ride off down the slope as if heading for the sheep flocks and the new deadline. Nick lost track of him among the lower trees.

He waited there, tired, hungry and thirsty through a long period. Behind him ran a gully where he had left his horse. Resting his aching eyes from the sun's relentless dazzle, he concentrated on what his ears could tell him. Presently he heard the low, inquiring whicker of his horse. Not long after that, he saw a small, careful stirring among the trees below him. He slid back then until cut from sight of the stage station. Rising to his feet, he dropped down to where his horse waited. Swinging to the saddle, he rode down the gulch, and around the first turn found himself looking at the drawn six-gun of a waiting Lacey.

The little killer had a wicked grin on his features. "Lose something you're looking for, Marquis?"

"Could have," Nick said.

"Chances are you'll find it down there." The gunman gestured to the stage station. "Maybe we'd better go down and look. You first."

Without a word Nick edged his horse past Lacey's on the narrow trail. The gunman's hand flicked out, lifting Nick's gun from its holster and Nick stiffened, his eyes genuinely hard on Lacey. He had no trouble feigning uneasiness—Lacey was gun-happy, and a dead Nick Marquis would suit him as well as a live one.

"Down the gulch, cowboy," Lacey ordered.

Nick rode ahead, remembering the last time he had been in Coyle's power. The latter might decide—as Nick hoped—that he had a hostage even more important than Laramie, but he also would have a few old scores to settle. The gulch soon fanned out onto the open plateau. He could hear Lacey's horse coming on steadily behind him. Just to keep the gunman persuaded that his capture had been genuine, Nick let his gaze prowl right and left as if hunting a chance to break away and ride for it.

Ten minutes later they rode into the stage station. Tripp Coyle was waiting in the yard, as was Pilar Corta. Looking at Pilar, Coyle said, "Didn't I tell you it'd be this ringy Marquis?" The Basque only shrugged. Nick saw no sign of Carlita. Coyle's *cocinero* had come to the door of the station building and was looking out. Beside this building there was the low-roofed barn, an open-sided shed, and something he had been unable to make out clearly from the distance, the slanted door of a root-cellar dug into the slope lifting behind the station. Ten to one that was Laramie's prison.

Nick gave the cellar door no overt attention,

drifting his sullen glance back to Tripp Coyle.

"What'll it be this time—another beating?" he asked.

"That depends, Marquis."

"On what?"

"On whether you ask for it. Throw him in with the old coot, Lacey."

Nick had trouble keeping his face angry and stiff. He hadn't dared to hope he would be put in direct contact with Laramie, although he had not fully realized the scanty accommodations here. At Lacey's order he swung down, at a gesture he walked toward the root cellar. Its low slanting doors, he noticed, were battened by a heavy bar. The gunman told him to swing up the bar, which Nick did, then he lifted the doors back. Light fell onto crumbling steps cut in the earth. As he went down he saw the dim interior of the cavelike, musty place. Laramie was stretched on blankets at one side, staring at him with disbelieving eyes. Then the doors shut behind him and the place was dark as night.

"How come you let 'em get hold of you again?" Laramie whispered after a moment.

Nick hunkered by him. "I teased them into it, Laramie. Are you all right?"

"So far. But I'd have come in for some rough treatment save for them Boscos. Nick, they're white men. I heard 'em arguing with Coyle about me having blankets and water and grub—if you can call cooked sheep grub. What's happened on the slope?"

"We've moved down to the lower rim, Laramie."

The old man groaned. "I knew that's what you boys'd do. Dunno what it'll buy, though. I wouldn't trust Coyle any more'n I would a coyote. Reckon we got a chance to bust out of here?"

"We can try. How do they feed you?"

"There's no chance of jumping anybody when they open them doors," Laramie answered. "The way they slant, one man at the top could knock over a dozen men trying to climb out. They open the doors, set grub on the steps, then bar the doors again. I'd be glad to have company if I didn't figure you're needed worse on the outside."

"Where's the girl?" Nick asked.

"I ain't seen her. Heard tell, though, she's lost some of her fancy for Coyle. He still wants her, though."

The answer heartened Nick. Carlita Corta was the weak link here—he could understand how she would be Coyle's weakness, too. Under the right conditions, she could be any man's. Nick felt his own blood quicken a little at the thought of her.

As his eyes adjusted to the darkness, he could see a little. Laramie had run out of tobacco and he rolled a smoke from Nick's supply. Then Nick pulled off his boots and loosened the tucked-in pants legs. He shook out the skinning knives he had placed under each before leaving Moccasin.

"Man!" Laramie breathed. "I allus said a man ought to carry some hideaway steel—though I never cottoned much to knives myself." The old man was grinning.

Nick, looking about for a place to hide the knives, saw an old empty barrel. Tipping the barrel, he laid the knives under it, then straightened the rickety old container again.

"Do they look in on you at night?"

"I don't hear anybody. But there's doubtless somebody around."

"Wouldn't be much of a trick to widen the cracks in those doors enough to let us work the bar loose."

"We can try," Laramie said. "But it's sure hard to tell in here when it's night outside."

In about an hour boots scraped outside the door. "Breakfast," said Laramie. Nick heard the bar pulled back from its seats. The doors opened. Lacey stood there at the head of the stairs while the Basque cook stepped down with plates of food and cups of coffee, which he placed on the steps.

"You got five minutes to get around it," Lacey called down.

The food was some kind of stew, which, because of his hunger, Nick ate with appetite.

He drank the coffee and put his plate and cup back on the step. When Laramie had finished the meal, he did likewise. The *cocinero* came to gather up the stuff, then the doors came shut again.

In the short period of light Nick had managed to locate the approximate position of the bar across the doors and fix it in his mind. He and Laramie smoked cigarettes in the resumed obscurity, the air growing musty and stale.

The long day wore past. No more food was brought until late afternoon. That time the *cocinero* had Laramie hand out a canteen, which was filled with fresh water. Lacey had nothing to say at all, no more taunts or jeering. Afterward jarred earth brought report of horsemen arriving. A little later they departed.

"Wonder if somebody come for more men?" Laramie remarked.

"Too much to hope for," Nick answered.

In that wearing darkness, minutes stretched into seeming hours. Yet they had to be sure they waited long enough before trying their luck at forcing the bar on the door. Nick knew that Laramie was sweating it out with him. Then something happened to help them judge the time—not far away a coyote howled.

Wordlessly, the two men came to their feet. The space under the shut doors was shallow, awkward, and they were forced to lie on their backs, work upward. Then began a patient business of scraping along the boards until each of them found a crack through which he could work his knife. They began to shave back and forth with the sharp skinning tools. The sound, because of the closeness and the small open space, was loud in their ears. Within minutes Nick was sweating profusely.

But the dried wood cut easily. As he got more room to work, it went faster. He could slide the knife easily, presently, for some six inches above the bar. Cutting in under the bar and then behind so the knife could be got in to push took more time. When he asked, "How are you doing?" Laramie grunted an affirmative answer.

Both of them knew that they might move out of this cave into instant death. Nonetheless they had to try it, and Nick worked furiously at the last whittling. Then all at once the bar moved without any pressure from either knife.

They both lay silent and panting, certain that somebody had heard the knives or seen their protruding tips. They both pulled down and swung about, still squatting as far under the doors as they could, ready to spring and stab.

Nick's half of the twin doors came open, and he surged up, knife raised, before he realized the figure above him wore a dress.

"Carlita!" he breathed and heard her hiss at him.

She came down the steps in an instant and let the door drop shut behind her.

"God, I nearly stabbed you!" Nick muttered.

"Just listen, Nick Marquis," she whispered. "There is little time. Some men came for Coyle and my brothers, but Lacey is here. He is in the station, drinking coffee to keep awake. I slipped out the window and came here. I'm going to let you go, Nick Marquis, and God forgive me for betraying my brothers."

"They still want to side with Coyle?"

"They have sworn the oath, Nick, to avenge the death of our father and take land from the cattlemen."

"I don't reckon any man's bound to go ahead with a deal he learns is wrong." Nick was thinking furiously, knowing how bad it would be for her if suspected of helping him, as she would be. Apparently in her haste she had not noticed that they were working on the door even as she opened it. "You go out and fasten that bar again, Carlita. We were about ready to open it ourselves. Slip back into the station and talk to Lacey or something to keep him interested. That's all we need and then you can't be blamed."

"If I must betray my brothers, I do not mean to be sly about it."

"Do what I say. Your brothers wouldn't hurt you, but Coyle might."

"Yes," she agreed with a sigh. "He has told me that if he cannot have me with my permission, he will have me without it. I am afraid of him, so I keep hidden when I can."

"Carlita, you've got to come with me."

"With you?"

"Yes. This is a poor place to say it, but when this trouble is over, there's nothing I want to do but take care of you."

All at once, and regardless of Laramie, she was sobbing in his arms. "Then you know why I do this thing."

"I know."

"But I cannot leave my brothers—"

"All right. Then go back in and keep Lacey tied up for a few minutes. They'll see how we got out of here just as soon as they find out we're gone. You won't be blamed."

He kissed her and felt the sweet, seeking response of her lips. Then she moved away from him. He saw a patch of sky as the door opened. He watched her slip through with an ache in his throat; then the door shut again.

"That's an all right gal," Laramie whispered.

"You never said truer, Laramie."

They waited five minutes. The bar, when they tried it again with their knives, moved easily. Perhaps Carlita had seen to it that it would. Very slowly and quietly, Nick lifted his half of the door. The stage yard about him was empty. He could see light in the stage station, and Carlita had thought to place herself where he could see her through a window. She was talking. Motioning to Laramie, Nick moved on out. It would be too noisy trying to rope horses out of the corral. He replaced the bar on the doors and he and Laramie slipped away on foot.

It was a long, hard walk for men with boots canted on riding heels, and twice they had to hide when they saw riders moving along the open space below them. "Something's up," Laramie had said the first time, and neither of them could make out what it was. They had to get down below the new deadline rim before daylight or an entire day of hiding in hostile country would be required, and the difficult travel left them few thoughts for anything else. Slowly, doggedly, they made their way down toward the rim above Moccasin.

They had nearly made it when, all at once, Nick grew aware that the low, crackling sound of which he had for a moment been aware was something important. Pulling up, he listened with hard intentness.

"Laramie," he gasped, "that's shooting!"

"It sure as hell is," Laramie agreed after a breath. "You reckon them sons of bitches have attacked the ranch?"

They pushed on heedlessly, then, forgetting discomfort, taking their chances. The sounds of the gunfire grew louder.

"It's Coyle's men that's been doing all the running around," Laramie breathed. "How the hell did they get them a fight at that place?"

Nick had no idea. Whatever had been maneuvered, Coyle and his men were occupied, permitting him and Laramie to move more openly. They veered to the west, came in upon the rim, and presently Nick could see the streaks of muzzle flame. Most of the shooting came from the top of the rim, but it was being returned in lesser but equally savage volume from the rocks below.

Nick wondered if somehow the cattlemen had got word of an intended raid and were trying to stop it here. That was the only thing that would explain this, and his helplessness galled him. In a hushed voice he said to Laramie, "We've got to get to the ranch, get horses and shooting irons and come back." At the old man's nod they retreated along the rim. Finally they made a sliding, reckless descent to the talus, then on down.

They did more running than walking from there on to Moccasin headquarters. The place seemed serene, a light burned in the house. "You saddle horses," Nick said to Laramie, "while I see if there's any guns left on the place."

He headed toward the house, and as his boot

heels thumped on the porch the door opened. Lily looked out anxiously.

She gasped. "Nick—your horse came in! Pat thought they'd caught you. He got men to help him sneak to Coyle's camp and try to free you and Laramie. I've been hearing shooting."

Nick swore. "Coyle must have sent my horse back, figuring Pat would investigate. Then he laid a gun trap for the rescue party—he'll say Pat tried to jump his sheep—" He pushed past Lily into the house. "Did Pat leave any guns around?"

All he could find in the way of firearms was a shotgun and an old hunting rifle of Pat's. By the time he stepped out into the yard, Laramie was coming up with horses. Nick swung to saddle, and they left the place at a sloping run.

They were halfway to the rim when the firing stopped. A little later they met riders—Pat, Simpson and four others. Pat had been wary enough not to be trapped wholly by Coyle's ambush, and when the fighting reached a stalemate, the cowmen had pulled out. They hadn't lost a man, and in the darkness it had been impossible to tell what Coyle's casualties were.

Back at the Moccasin, Lily had a big pot of hot coffee ready. After a while, Pat said in a tired voice, "That tramp's sure handed us a tough one. Now that he's got the Lilyville sheepers backing him, he's got men enough to hit us both at home and on the deadline—even if we tried to get the deadline back. Nick, you've come up with some good answers before. I sure hope you've got one now."

Nick shook his head wearily. "The man throws his punches too damned fast."

"He's got his own weaknesses," Herb Simpson growled.

Nick kept shaking his head. "Hitting his sheep wouldn't hold him in check now. He's got men enough to guard them as well as to harry us till we throw in the sponge."

"Damn Ray Morton," Simpson breathed. "No, me and Ryder Ives didn't have to listen to him that day up in Boulder when he preached the idea of not fighting Coyle unless he broke his promise to let us alone. A man can sure sell himself arguments in line with what he hopes for. Me and Ryder did, the same as Ray. And we're responsible for this damned situation."

Simpson and his riders left presently, heading for Gooseneck. Shortly thereafter dawn began to run its milky tinge into the eastern horizon. And with it came a man's hail from the ranchyard.

It was Pilar Corta.

Nick and Pat had come to the porch. Pilar had a rifle in his saddle boot, a knife in his belt, but he looked more uncertain than hostile.

"I have been waiting, *señores*," he said. "And I have not long. I must talk to Nick Marquis."

Nick understood that the Basque had been

hiding in the sagebrush, waiting for the Gooseneck men to leave.

"Swing down, Pilar," he invited.

"No, *señor*, I must go." There was a new respect in the man's voice now. He made a sibilant sucking of breath past strong white teeth. "My sister she tell me that she betray me and Tomas, but it is not so. It is Tomas and Pilar who nearly betray their sister. She tell me she love you, *señor*, but that is not what make the difference. It is that Tomas and I have learn that the sheep king he is as bad as the cattle king. Tripp Coyle, he is resolve to have this slope, to make himself the sheep king of the West. That he tell us when we demand that he turn over to us our own sheep."

"I'm glad you see the light, Pilar," Nick said, and Pat smiled at the Basque.

"I have the trouble with the words," Pilar went on. "But it is like this. Tomas and Pilar would like to help keep Coyle from becoming the sheep king that is as bad as the cattle king. You understand?"

Nick did. The Cortas had fought for revenge because it was a point of honor to their kind. Like Ray Morton, they had let themselves trust imponderables out of the urgency of their own desires. But they had something more than Morton possessed—the courage to acknowledge fault and make amends.

"So, Pilar?" Nick asked.

For the first time Corta smiled. "So maybe

we can fix this Coyle. It is only possible, and it will be very hard. But my Basques can handle the sheep better than any other men. Maybe something can happen to those sheep, *señores*, that will be for their good instead of hurting them."

"I don't get it," Pat said, shaking his head.

"Coyle need all the fighting men he can get," Pilar explained. "He plan the big raid. It is to be tomorrow night. Every cattle ranch below him, it is to be struck. Yet how would it profit him if when he gained land he had not sheep for it?"

"Pilar, can you do it?" Nick breathed.

The Basque let out a gusty sigh. "It is only the small possibility. But now you know that tomorrow night you must fight for your homes. It may be that you cannot save them. I do not know. But the minute Coyle's men are well started, the sheep they will start moving. Toward Utah, as you have said. If you can make him busy for the length of the night, the flocks will be past a new line—trapped where you can hold them again. Without grass unless the sheep keep moving toward the Utah railroad. Can do?"

"Can try," Nick answered.

"Then I go," Pilar said, and he swung his horse and rode off, soon vanishing into the rock and sage.

"That surprised the hell out of me," Pat reflected. "Reckon he's telling the truth?"

"I think so. I thought from the first it was only a matter of time before the Basques broke with Coyle—and the Cortas ain't dumb. Don't discount what he said about our chances being mighty slim."

"How many men do you estimate Coyle's got now?" Pat asked.

"Not enough that he could throw a very big party against any one ranch," Nick told him. "He's counting on surprise, which is where Pilar's been a big help, already. I know that 'line' he's talking about—it's a row of hills south on the stage road. The Basques would need a good eight or ten hours to trail past it. Which means that much fighting for us if they're to get away with it."

"But if it works," Pat said grimly, "we've got the devil licked."

"If it works," Nick agreed.

They decided that Pat and the two oldsters, Bike and Laramie, should carry the warning along the slope at once. Each ranch was to prepare itself for a long siege, not driving off possible attackers before the required time even if that proved possible. One ranch hand Nick detailed to follow Pilar Corta and to keep an eye on developments at the stage station from a distance.

Restless as Nick was, he knew that Pat's counsel of sleep was wise in face of what lay ahead of them all. When the men had ridden out with the warning, Nick sat down to the breakfast Lily had fixed for him. She was very quiet, pale of face.

"You still love Pace," Nick told her bluntly as he began to eat. "And you're worried about him."

After a moment, she said, "I guess you're right on both scores. I loved him too much in the beginning. Too much ever to forget him."

"He told me about his having wanted to be a preacher."

She looked at him fiercely. "He could have been a great man, but something went wrong inside him. He renounced everything. I was wrong to crowd him. After he vanished, I knew it. But also I thought I hated him for giving me up. Hate's an awful thing, Nick—a spreading rot."

"Still you followed him."

"Not exactly. I vanished, too. I thought he'd turned against everything decent and good, and I tried. I came here. Then one day he stopped at my place for a room. Then he took a job on Wing I and stayed."

"A lot of years."

"About five. Nick, what is that thing in a person that can be very good or very bad?"

Nick said thoughtfully, "Maybe it's just two sides of the same thing—depending on where you stand when you look at it."

Lily said slowly, "Pace reached a point where he didn't think there was any good side at all.

And I sold women in my place, Nick. I did it deliberately. A kind of revenge against myself, I think, for being a woman."

"Why don't you go back to him, Lily?" Nick said gently.

"What's there left? He's not the man I married, nor am I the woman he did."

"I hope to God you're wrong."

Nick managed to sleep for a few hours. When he roused and came out of the bunkhouse, Pat, Bike and Laramie were still gone. Lily was about but avoided being alone with him, and he realized she did not want to talk to him again. Perhaps she regretted what she had admitted, yet on the other hand, he thought, talking had been good for her.

He was washing up at the bunkhouse when he saw two riders coming in from the west. As the horses drew nearer, he stiffened in sudden, hard attention. A moment later he could identify old Quince in the lead.

Nick went pounding across the yard to meet them. Quince Acton stared down at him with dull, tired eyes. Pace Erskine was behind, bloody from his waist to his boot-tops, swaying in the saddle.

Nick asked, "Where's Bronco and Andy?"

Quince worked his mouth as if it were very dry. "Dead. Both of 'em. Them bastards cornered us finally. Fought most of yesterday. Nobody left by night but me and Pace. We broke away in the dark."

Lily was coming across the sun-bronzed earth, her face stricken. Pace mumbled, "Lily," and would have toppled from the saddle had not Nick caught him as he fell.

Nick walked toward the ranchhouse with the man. They placed Pace on a couch in the front room. The wound was in his side, and he had lost so much blood his skin was like dried parchment. He had lost consciousness.

Nick said, "It's up to you, Lily. We can't spare a man to go for a doc. The closest one is at Albion."

She was already starting.

Quince came in by the time Nick got the clothes off Pace. Together they applied a crude bandage, washed the blood from his lower body and got him to bed. Quince, with the sure hand of long experience, had freshened the fire and was heating sadirons that in the long ago Pat's wife had used. These they put in beside the man to bring warmth to his deeply shocked body. Finally Nick forced Pace's mouth open and got him to swallow some whisky.

That was all they could do until Lily got there with the doctor. Before then the ranch must undergo and somehow survive Tripp Coyle's attack. Nick shook his head—Quince was dead on his feet and needed sleep, but there were things Nick had to know first.

"That means the local sheepers will be down here to help Coyle," he said.

Pace nodded, a mere numbed tip of the head. "Wanting to is what turned 'em so wild. Burned out Lily Falcone, which was like blood scent to a bunch of Injuns. They had to be in on the kill down here next. They got parties in on all sides of us, and finally pinned us down."

"Get to bed, Quince. Got word this morning that Coyle's hitting every ranch on this part of the slope tonight. With the help he's going to have now, we'll need every man's gun."

12

Pat, Laramie and Bike were not back until late afternoon. Quince was up by then, and he and Pat came in to where Nick sat by Pace's bed.

Pat's main concern as always was for his men. "How is he?" he asked.

"Still holding on, and that's all I know, Pat. Lily went for a doctor, but she can't be back before tomorrow."

"By then," Pat said harshly, "we could all be dead. I've got to warn the other ranchers it'll be a lot tougher than we thought."

"Send Quince to Gooseneck and have Herb Simpson spread the word. You're worn out, and Quince has had a little rest."

Pat went out. Nick felt wholly useless sitting there with Pace, yet he could not bring himself to leave the man. A lonely man, he knew now, with tragedy locked in his heart, a man of disillusionment and more recently of regret.

It wouldn't do any good, but something made him say quietly, "Pace, Lily told me she still loves you."

By some miracle, Pace seemed to hear. His bloodless lips worked, trying to answer. Assured that he was being heard, perhaps as if in a dream, Nick said it again. Medicine, he thought, just what Pace needs. He kept saying it.

He realized presently that instead of lying there in that dying half-consciousness, Pace was sleeping, resting.

Nick went out quietly. Pat had sent Quince off and returned to the porch, where he sat disconsolately on the top step. Nick seated himself, pulled out tobacco and rolled a cigarette.

"Pat," he said, when he had fired the smoke, "with help from Lilyville, Coyle will swamp us sure. Are you willing to gamble on a bluff?"

"It's a gamble any way you look at it," Pat said. "What's the bluff?"

"Wish I'd thought of it before Quince left, but I was thinking about Pace. It's ten to one every land-hungry sheeper up there will be here by the time Coyle moves tonight. He might have sent for them, even. We might be burned out either way, but we don't need to get wiped out with it."

"What's the difference?"

"As long as a man's got his life he can build over. Suppose those sheepers ride in on empty buildings, not a man around to fire a shot at them?"

"They'd have 'em a party," Pat spat.

"Maybe not, Pat. They'd be sure to look around first. Supposing they found a notice tacked on the door for them at each place, saying thanks for the sheep?"

Pat stared at him in hard wonder. "Looks like

that'd louse up the Boscos' plans, except I think you have more in mind."

"You bet," Nick said vehemently. "They'd know we'd been tipped off, and since the Basques have been dissatisfied a long while, Coyle would guess who did it. But he'd be below the rim and us on top, with it easy to keep them down there and a lot less costly to us. The gamble is that they might not even take time to fire our buildings, they'd be so anxious to see what in hell was happening to their sheep. That way we could make sure we held them off long enough for the Cortas to get the sheep down south of that line, the way we want."

"I've bet on worse hands than that," Pat said. "I'm game."

"Then I'd better get to Gooseneck before Herb sends men around."

"Get going."

The prospect of fighting like something other than trapped animals energized Nick, letting him throw off his jading fatigue as, presently, he rode east toward Gooseneck. Quince was still there. Simpson and his men were saddling horses.

"Hold 'em a minute, Herb," Nick said.

Simpson passed the order, then looked at Nick inquiringly. "Don't tell me something else has gone wrong."

"That's one comfort, Herb—things can't get much worse." Nick went on to explain what he had talked over with Pat. Simpson's eyes showed a gleam as he listened; none of them had relished the thought of a desperate, pinned-down fight against long odds.

Simpson turned to the men waiting with saddled horses by the corral fence. "You all heard. Have you got it straight?" He asked Nick, "Where do they rally, Nick?"

Nick told them and the riders left, splitting, each carrying the word to a different ranch. Nick didn't worry that this activity was probably being observed by Coyle's spies. The more uneasy the sheepmen were when they started their foray onto the lower slope, the more quickly would they react to the suggestion that they had been tricked.

Nick returned to Moccasin with Quince. Pace Erskine was still sleeping peacefully and his cheeks showed more color. The will to live has a powerful influence over the human body, and maybe Pace had that will again.

Although Quince protested, Nick assigned him to help move Pace to a line cabin, out of harm's way, and to stay with the wounded man. Quince had had fighting enough for a while. That left four of them, himself, Pat, Laramie and Bike, to join Simpson's half-dozen men at the notch directly south of Moccasin. Herb had said they would be there shortly after nightfall, and the Moccasin men got their guns and ammunition ready. Laramie fixed a meal and insisted that they eat it.

An hour after dark they saddled and rode out. By then the first stars were emerging. Ten men moved a little west of Moccasin headquarters before turning south toward the night-shrouded rim, taking care to conceal themselves in the natural cover. They came in close to the notch that was their objective, dismounted and settled to wait.

Soon the faint wild sounds of the night were all that seemed to be about them. Coyle's sheep were too far back from the rim to be heard. Nick's fatigues settled on him, the body's limitations insistent against the demand of the mind. He wanted to smoke but couldn't risk it.

Then, perhaps an hour later, a horseman broke boldly over the rim and started down through the notch.

The sight swept all weariness from Nick again. One by one other riders followed, breaking over and moving down. He could count them easily in the moment in which they were backlighted against the starlit sky, and there had been fifteen when they stopped showing themselves up there. At the lower edge of the cleft, by then, men had bottomed out and were moving onto the flatter ground. They went on in a group, but Nick knew that very soon they would split into three bunches to carry the attack to Moccasin, Gooseneck and

B Bar B. He was positive that at each of the other notches the same thing was taking place.

Nick said quietly, "They're down, Pat. Come on."

"See the sheep king?" Pat asked. "Coyle?"

"I think so. He'd pick you and me for his meat, wouldn't he?"

Pat made a sound of satisfaction.

They rode quietly toward the notch, single file, then emerged from the lower cover and entered the constricted climb to the top of the rim that was a sharp black line against the stars. There they moved their horses back to a safe distance, picketed the animals and returned to the battle line. Nick split the men evenly, putting five on each side of the descent. Again they settled to silence.

It was not an easy wait, and Nick's gaze kept straying out toward Moccasin, then Gooseneck and on, dreading to see the first rosy tinge of flames. As yet he saw nothing but opaque distances.

There was no mistaking it when the first riders swept back. Those who had gone in to Moccasin were first, and Nick saw them all at once as their running horses broke into view. Their heedlessness and confusion were betrayed when they did not think to probe the notch, instead driving on toward it, expecting that the sheep already were being slaughtered by the hundreds.

Nick opened fire, saw a horse rear up, throwing its rider. Along the rim at either hand guns joined in, rifles at this point, speaking savagely and ruthlessly. It was a fight to the end now.

The oncoming riders wheeled in confusion. A second later the bunch exploded outward, scattering to the nearest cover. Nick could hear somebody shouting urgently and was certain he recognized Coyle's heavy, carrying voice. This gratified him almost as much as if he had been present when the self-appointed sheep king read the note of thanks tacked on Pat's door. No buildings would be burned tonight. Coyle's whole concern was for his investment, his sheep.

A hot return fire was soon coming out of the rocks and sagebrush below. The bullets impacted on the rimrock to shrill angrily into the night. Some passed overhead, but the angle of the slope favored the cattlemen. Coyle would in time try to pull back and flank the rim, but he would not choose the long ride required while he thought he could drive through. No fires had broken out in the greater distance, which meant that his two other parties were in all probability already flogging back.

A little later Nick saw riders sweep in on a slant from Gooseneck. The situation was fully revealed to them by the time they pulled up out of range and swung down. They came running in, a figure now and then disclosing itself in the gaps between rock and sage. The effect of their added fire was instantly apparent. Again Coyle's encouraging shouts rang out.

Gradually the intensity of the firing subsided as men reloaded and sought new positions. Those on the rim continued their more cautious relay firing, which never for a moment permitted the enemy to grow careless.

The third party came driving across the sage-studded, flattened plateau toward the contested rim gap. It went into action the same as the others, wheeling up, dismounting and footing it in. Now Coyle called for a charge.

He had men enough to bring it off, Nick knew. They didn't rise to make a rush of it, lacking the numbers for that, but he could tell from the way the shooting came closer that they were all working forward toward the talus. Once more the firing increased in tempo. It was two or three minutes before Nick was sure the sheepmen, whether or not Coyle liked it, had lost their drive.

The abortive rush apparently had taken much of the enthusiasm out of Tripp Coyle's men. The firing remained brisk, steady, but it was more judicious. The night wore away with its savagery undiminished. Nick knew that Coyle was confronted by a decision. The strength here at the gaps would have told him that if an attack had been made on his sheep it could not have been in force. Whatever harm could be done had been done. The only remaining question was whether to press this costly effort to break onto the rim immediately or try the very long way around in a flanking movement.

In the predawn hour, Nick grew aware that the sheepmen were pulling out. The reduced firing from below became apparent, although they were careful as they withdrew and remained so when they reached their horses and rode out.

Nick began crawling to the right to where Pat Tracer was stationed. The old man made a motion toward the belowground and said, "They've had enough for now. What's our next move?"

"He'll split this party," Nick reflected, "and send half each way to pick up the sheepmen at the other gaps. Then they'll go on around, leaving enough men to keep us tied down here. Pilar said they'd start moving the sheep as soon as Coyle had his men out of sight. By now they ought to be well on their way. By the time Coyle can cut around with enough men, the Basques ought to have the sheep where Pilar promised. I say we'd better clear out now, catch up with the Cortas and ride guard on them. Then we can concentrate on holding that line instead of this."

Pat agreed. It was necessary for them to pick up their own men at the other gaps also. Meanwhile, Nick inspected the damage—old Bike had had his cheek cut deeply by a rock splinter; he was the only casualty so far.

The shooting from below was soon so desultory it was evident that only three or four men had been left here.

Nick said, "I'll catch up with the Cortas, Pat, and warn them of what might be coming at them. You can afford another hour here to gather the rest of the boys. Then come on up to the sheep."

He was soon in the saddle, riding south. Daylight was strong across the plateau by then. He saw that the sheep grounds were empty. The Basques had carried out their part of the agreement. The flocks were beyond the deserted stage station when he got there, and even the sheepwagon had been driven off. He paused a moment.

A sight worth seeing would be Coyle's face when he discovered what had actually happened to his sheep. He would fight furiously to regain possession of them, but now the animals would be a help to the cattlemen, who could hold them as hostages to be destroyed. But Coyle still had thirty or forty men against possibly half that many cattlemen, and might conceivably increase those odds. Nick had long since learned the utter folly of too much confidence. He pressed on in the broad wake of one of the flocks. He could tell from the close packing of their tracks how steadily they had been hurried. Basques were expert at that sort of thing. If anybody could get the animals to the south rim in time, they could.

And they would have won themselves a place

in this country, from which a great many of the avaricious sheepmen now would certainly be driven. That was a goal to fight for—and for Nick it included a girl whose eyes were black and shining, who was made for loving . . .

Judging by what had happened when he had last seen her, he had that kind of luck, if only it held through the next bitter hours.

13

He had not been south of the stage station in a long while. Presently the country narrowed into a broad coulee whose rugged walls showed a thicker growth of cedar and nut pine. The sheep had moved steadily, and as he remembered the situation hereabouts they still had an hour or two of travel to get below the line of the hills Pilar had mentioned.

He heard the sheep before he saw them. They had been brought into one immense band, strung out enormously. A mounted Basque rifleman was in the rear. His horse wheeled promptly and Nick saw the rifle come up to ready. A foot herder and his dog were handling the drag of the band and these were nearly lost in the dust that boiled up from the thousands of hoofs. Nick waved his hat in the universal gesture of friendliness. The rifle lowered, and the man motioned for him to come on.

He was not one of the Corta brothers but a Basque Nick had seen in the background before. Apparently he had been told to expect friends as well as foes, for while he looked concerned he showed no hostility.

"Something he is wrong, *señor*?" he asked.

"Not so far," Nick said. "Where's Pilar?"

The man nodded forward.

Nick rode on. He picked the less dusty side of the flock, but this was bad enough. He passed two herders. The strung-out sheep seemed to be unending. The chirming of their hoofs, their throaty wailing laid a deadly monotonous beat upon his ears. The coulee widened, but the band loosened with it to get more room. Finally the ridges stopped, and the sheep were fanning out on the south slope of the great plateau.

The two Cortas were in the lead. They did not see Nick until he had come clearly out of the floating dust. They also showed an instant wariness before they recognized him. Then Pilar lifted a friendly hand. Nick rode on up to them.

"We are nearly there," Pilar said. "Maybe another hour. What has happen, *señor*?"

Nick told them, explaining how he had changed tactics to make sure the sheep could travel without molestation as long as possible, as well as increasing the cattlemen's chances in the hot, deadly fight. Pilar's gleaming eyes showed his approval of that and Tomas smiled.

"Where's Carlita?" Nick concluded.

"She and Manuel went ahead with the wagon," Pilar said. "By now they are below the line. You think Coyle have the time to give us trouble before we get the sheep there?"

"He could make it," Nick warned. "But my men should be along before his. Now that you know,

I'll fall back to the rear. As soon as the cattlemen come up, I'll fan them out on both sides. If Coyle hits before then, I guess it's just our tough luck."

"The luck she has been running good so far," Pilar answered. "And if we must we will run the sheep over some ledge, which is a thing we much hate."

Nick swung to higher ground for his return ride, not only to get out of the dust but because, if Coyle got around faster than expected, there would be a chance of seeing him come in. But he reached the rear without incident, and made contact with the Basque there.

"This," the man said, "is what we should have done one long time ago."

"Better late than never," Nick said.

They rode along silently. Nick knew that if Coyle got ahead of the cattlemen he would not attack the sheep themselves but would try to overpower the herders. In that case Nick had no doubt that Pilar would do what he threatened. Sheep were thoroughly imitative creatures. If the Cortas lifted the lead animals into a run and piled them over a ledge, the rest would follow to the last sheep.

Nothing had happened to change the monotonous pattern when Pat rode up with the cattlemen, a good thirty of them now that they were united, but fewer men by far than Coyle had at his disposal. Nick at once divided them, sending them down the flanks of the big sheep band, the rear of which was still in the long coulee. He felt easier after that, although there was still a considerable distance to travel.

Pat took the west ridge, Nick the east, and they left the sheep. They meant to patrol the far sides, and if either saw the enemy he would fire three shots as a warning signal. That would enable the others to take defensive positions along the flanks of the flock, close enough for every shot a sheepman fired to endanger the sheep as well.

Not far past the ridgeline the pine and cedar thinned out. Nick had barely reached this edge of the growth when he saw riders far down on the slope. They were driving their horses with brutal savagery, and he judged that there were about thirty of them, with a smaller force coming in from the other direction.

Lifting his rifle, Nick fired three shots and not only as a signal, for he sent them straight at the oncoming party.

The shrilling bullets scattered them but they came on, scarcely missing stride. It was wholly useless to try to hold up so many of them here, and Nick wheeled his horse and sent it driving back into the trees. Cutting in and out through the timber, he rode on a southeastern tangent, wanting to come in ahead of the flock. He had barely pounded onto the slope above the rimrock when shooting broke out all along the line behind him. The cattlemen, warned by the signal, had met the assault with speedy determination.

He saw Pilar and Tomas still leading their precious charges, cool about it, not letting themselves be stampeded into brash action.

Nick called to them, "No need to sacrifice the critters yet! My boys are along both sides!"

Pilar nodded, and Nick rode on. About a mile later he came to the abrupt drop-off of the rim. This formation ran like a long dam between two mountain masses, a skillfully selected barrier. But he was thinking of the sheepwagon now that Coyle was so close at hand. He wanted Carlita and Manuel to abandon it and reach some point of safety.

He hit the grade down from the rim at a clatter, seeing the wheel tracks of the wagon. A mile farther on he saw the wagon halted in the middle of the road and knew a strange, choking sensation. When he came on around he saw a dead mule lying in its harness. The wagon was deserted. The other animals were gone.

"Carlita!" he yelled. "Manuel!" He knew already that they weren't here. Even so, he jerked open the back door of the wagon for a look at the empty interior. He climbed to the driver's seat and his sick feeling deepened. There was blood on the seat.

Coyle must have found tracks to show that the wagon was ahead, although the Cortas had relied on the massed hoofs of the band to obliterate them. The man had sent someone ahead who had been able to stop the wagon by shooting a mule and probably the driver. Carlita was in Coyle's hands, or those of one of his men.

All that flashed through Nick's mind as he raked the ground about him. Now that he looked for them, he noticed the bootprints, of two different sizes. The small ones sent a name drilling through his stunned thoughts—Lacey.

Coyle did not need to worry too much if he failed to stop the sheep from being moved down below the barrier.

Circling, Nick found the tracks of two horses. Probably the mules were broken to ride and had been used to spirit Carlita and Manuel away. He wished desperately that he knew which of them had left blood on the wagon seat. Yet he dared not let himself think along lines like that. Not now. His question was whether to trail Lacey and his companion, which might only endanger the captured Basques if they were still alive. Her safety required a more carefully considered plan than that.

He was soon racing back toward the rim, then up the grade to the top. Just as he broke over he saw the sheep coming up. The Cortas had thinned the leaders into a point, which they were managing toward the grade. Nick could not ride in on them without breaking up that delicate movement. He pulled down his heaving horse, stunned by a sense of complete defeat.

He grew aware for the first time that the distant shooting had stopped. Perhaps the sheepmen realized that too hard-pressed an attack now might precipitate a sheep run over the rim. Maybe Coyle had learned already that he still held the high cards. The trained leaders hit the grade and started down, the following sheep moving behind them obediently. Soon the whole vast mass was pouring over, like water over a spillway.

When the movement was well started, Pilar rode over to Nick, grinning until he saw the stricken look on Nick's features.

"Something has gone wrong?"

"Yeah, Pilar. They caught the wagon."

"Carlita!" Pilar said. "What is it with my sister?"

"They've got her, Pilar. Coyle will give you a chance to trade the sheep for her."

Fury flushed into the whitened face of the man. "When you play with the devil," he breathed, "you pay the price. I will kill him, Nick Marquis, and I will not kill him easy."

"I promised myself that privilege a long while ago," Nick said. "But we can't rush into it. We'll get the sheep down there and our men on the rim. Then wait for him to make contact. He will."

"There is no doubt of that, *amigo*."

Silent and tense, they sat watching the sheep pour down the grade. Nick could see the leaders fanning out below. The first herders came up, and Pilar motioned them aside, telling them to go no farther.

It seemed to take an hour for all the sheep to reach the rim and go down. By then the accompanying guard and herders made a sizable contingent on the rim. As they came up they learned what had happened to take the savor from this moment. Grimly furious, they waited there until the last sheep had flicked over the edge and onto the grade.

Pat Tracer stared hard at Nick. "I sure hope you ain't reached the bottom of the barrel, man," he said.

"Just about," Nick admitted. "We're never allowed to forget this isn't a white man's war. If Coyle can wind it up without trading back the girl, I think he'd like to keep her."

The men watched him intently for the orders he found hard to shape up. He said, "Pilar, this is as tough for me as for you and Tomas. Even if we kept our half of a bargain Coyle might offer, he wouldn't give us back Carlita. You know that as well as we do from his record. So we won't even wait for the offer to trade."

"What, then?" Pilar asked. His cheeks were ashen but he was in agreement.

"It's got to be a finish fight, here and now.

Afterward, we'll see what's left for you and me to do."

"It is the only thing to do," Pilar said, and Tomas nodded.

Looking at the others, Nick said briskly, "Coyle's up in the woods there getting ready to nail us down against the rim. We'll fool him. I want half a dozen volunteers to stay here to keep them from getting down. I want the rest of you to go on now. Start those sheep moving south again. If we have to take them clear into Utah, we'll do it. Meanwhile, Pilar and I will see what we can do to help Carlita and Manuel. That agreeable?"

Every man assented readily.

Herb Simpson wanted to hold the grade with his men and a couple from B Bar B. The others rode down the grade, Nick and the Cortas going along. The Basques quickly got the sheep organized and moving again. Once the movement was started, Pilar left the lead and rode over to where Nick sat his horse, watching.

"Now," he breathed. "What do you think we can do, Nick?"

"Coyle knows by now that his having Carlita won't buy him anything. Meanwhile, he's not going to let those sheep get out of his sight again if he can help. Once he finds out the grade's blocked, he won't waste time there, like he did at the north rim. He'll cut around, and it'll be a lot shorter ride this time. Then it's going to be another fight."

"You think we should wait and help?"

Nick shook his head. "I know where to pick up Lacey's sign, and we'll trail him to wherever he went."

He and Pilar cut through the rock and sagebrush again until they cut Lacey's sign. It led west, indicating that the man might have made for the hills in that direction, intending to thread them and get back to his own party.

Lacey had traveled rapidly. But, since there had been no attempt to foul the trail, it was easy to follow. The stalkers lifted their horses to a faster gait. Presently the outlying rises of the hills began to pass by them. Lacey had headed into a long climbing ravine. At its top he had turned north, confirming Nick's guess that he was trying to reach Coyle with his trophies.

About halfway along the side of the mountain at the west end of the rim, they came upon the body of Manuel. It lay carelessly beside Lacey's trail, and sight of it brought a ripping oath from Pilar as they rode up to it.

Pilar breathed, "They toss him aside like the dead dog! Ah!"

They swung down for a moment. Manuel's flesh was still warm but no trace of life remained in him. He had been shot through the chest. They moved the body into the shade of a stunted pine, where Pilar removed his hat for a moment.

"Manuel he love my sister," he said quietly. "It was to try to help her that he kept living this long. It is a thing to remember. This is a thing to avenge."

"We'd better go, Pilar," Nick said softly.

It was only a little while after that when Pilar pulled up his horse. "Listen!" he whispered. His ears were keener than Nick's, who did not until then detect the distant drum of fast-moving horses. "They are coming, Nick. We must hide and watch."

Nick agreed. Swinging off Lacey's trail, they moved higher onto the mountainside. There in a rock crop they swung down, moved to the heads of their horses to keep them quiet, and waited. In a matter of minutes riders broke into the clearing they had just left. Nick judged them to be the whole sheep contingent, massed now for the final test.

"There is Carlita!" Pilar hissed. "They make her ride with them!"

"Coyle knew we'd try for her," Nick said. "He didn't want to trust her to a small guard."

"What we do?"

"Does Coyle understand Basque?"

Pilar shook his head. "Few *anglos* can learn the tongue."

"Then we'll cut in ahead and let them pass close to us. You call to her to break and ride for it toward us. They won't shoot her. You know what Coyle wants."

"I know."

Pilar knew more than that, just as Nick did. Their chances of surviving such an effort were small indeed. Yet, without it, neither of them might ever see her again.

They cut down through the pines, driving their horses at a breakneck gait. They reached a point where the sheepmen would be slowed down by the need to climb a rough ridge. Keeping saddle with Pilar, Nick waited. They both held rifles in readiness. The first riders passed below them, putting their horses in single file up the ridge and forcing the whole line behind to rein in.

Then Pilar's carrying voice rang out, briefly, melodiously, urgently.

Every man in the party swung a startled look about. Carlita acted like a released spring. Her kneed horse jerked the reins out of its leader's hands, she gathered them in and rammed through the riders surrounding her.

Men milled in confusion. Carlita broke through. When three or four recovered and started after her, quick shots from the two rifles on the ridge side drove them back. Nobody shot at her, and Carlita made a beautiful ride, cutting her horse to the rear and clinging to its off side like an Indian, further protecting herself. The sheepmen had spotted the men above them and concentrated on them, perhaps figuring they could pick up the girl later.

Shooting steadily, Nick began to pull back along the ridge with Pilar, Carlita was climbing now onto the slope. They met her just as she rimmed out of the canyon. Nobody needed to speak, all three knowing they had a desperate ride to make to get away. Yet Carlita's eyes spoke for a flashing second of her gratitude to the men. She had probably been told what Coyle had in store for her in return for her defection.

They kept to the ridge top, cutting through the pine, forcing Coyle, if he pursued, to move away from his sheep. For a while the sheepmen did that; then they began to realize they were being decoyed away. The sounds of pursuit faded, but Nick kept his companions riding with him for another five minutes.

Pulling down to blow their winded horses, Nick said, "You all right, Carlita?"

"Yes," she said, but tears sprang into her eyes. "But poor Manuel. They just—"

"We know," Nick said. "Did you hear anything about what Coyle intends?"

She nodded, fighting back her grief. "I hear him explain it. They will pull ahead of the flock and hit it from in the front. That, Coyle explain, will let them shoot down the sides instead of into the sheep and over them. He know from what you do that you will not trade the sheep for me."

"I hope you understand that," Nick said.

"I prayed you would not be deceived into trusting him. Because he boasted that he would not only have his sheep back tonight but would be sharing the bed with me."

It took an hour for them to come out of the lower hills. They emerged at a point well back of the trailing sheep, and Nick's one comfort was that Pat and his men expected to be hit. No matter what happened, Coyle could not surprise them.

At the edge of the hills, Nick pulled his pistol and handed it to Carlita, saying, "Herb Simpson and his men are on the grade to the rim. Tell him Coyle's slipped around him. They're to come on to help us, and you are to keep riding. Go to Moccasin. You know how to find it."

"I know, Nick."

The fatigued sheep had not traveled fast. Half an hour later the simmering plateau showed them dust in the far foreground. Minutes later they heard the sound of gunfire.

A running, open fight was taking place ahead. The cattlemen had no desire to retain possession of the band when there was a chance to mix it freely with the sheepmen. Not only the old resentments drove them but all the things that had happened in this outbreak. Nick saw swirling clouds of dust, heard the punch of cracking guns as he asked his horse for its utmost.

His rifle was snug to his shoulder as he went

in. Ahead he saw Bike Johnson throwing savage shots at two sheepmen who were dogging him. Nick's cracking weapon emptied a saddle; Bike cleared the other sheepmen from leather. The old man let out a whoop as he flung a look at Nick. All about the trembling, piling flock, shambles was taking place.

Charging along with Bike on one side, Pilar on the other, Nick swept toward a group of half a dozen sheepmen who were trying to get the sheep moving, hoping to edge them over and out of harm's way. They swung their horses and began shooting. The three riders charging toward them never swerved. Bike's lips were peeled back in the grin of a fierce old man who stood to die with his boots on and preferred it that way. A sheepman's horse reared up and went over backward, pinning its rider as it came down. Another man threw both hands in the air, not in surrender but in a dying reflex before he toppled out of the saddle. Nick heard the scream of a bullet past his ear, almost heating his flesh. He saw hair clipped from between the ears of his horse and wondered how the bullet had ever passed his own body. But also he saw the last sheepman in that little party spill out of leather as the three riders swept on past.

The next pair were Canfield and Lacey and, seeing them, Pilar let out an Indian-like scream. The pair had come upon a cowman thrown from a wounded horse. They were potting shots at the man who was disputing them waspishly from behind the body of the horse. At Pilar's scream the gunmen swung their mounts. They jerked up their guns to fire again, and it was poetic justice to Nick to see the team that had worked so devilishly together quit leather in simultaneous falls.

Nick caught a riderless horse and took it to the downed man, who proved to be Bud Adair of B Bar B. Adair swung aboard, making them a foursome. Brisk shooting forward and rearward, as well as across the flock, proved that things were far from settled elsewhere. The four rode on.

They came upon Tomas Corta, whose horse had been dropped. Swinging back, Nick caught another with an empty saddle and brought it up. From the fact that the drawn look had gone from Tomas's face when he got back, Nick knew Pilar had told him that their sister was safe. Five men swept on.

Coyle and his surviving men were still fighting desperately for possession of the sheep. Ahead, through dust so thick it seemed to be early night, Nick could see riders and horses cutting about, their blazing guns making dirty scarlet streaks about them. Nick finished emptying his rifle as he drove through the fight and he pulled out to reload.

The hot weapon was barely recharged with ammunition when he saw three men trying to quit the fight together. He was at once in hot pursuit. His first shot swung a man about in the saddle. Another man fired at him but with a pistol, which seemed to be the only weapon he had. Then their fresher horses outdistanced him. They kept going.

The tide had turned. As the firing lessened in intensity a man wholly berserk came charging out of the dust. In the fury of his frustration, Tripp Coyle shot a fleeing sheepman out of the saddle. He swung his horse about in angry stubbornness, saw Nick, and dug in the spurs.

Nick was waiting eagerly, coolly. Coyle roared like an enraged bull as he lifted his saddle gun to shoulder and fired. Nick heard the bullet scream close to him as his rifle answered. His had been the cooler aim. For a moment Coyle only dropped the carbine and grabbed leather. His dust-streaked face looked surprised. He tumbled to the ground, rolled over once and was still.

Within five minutes there was nothing to hear but the nervous bleating of the sheep.

As the dust cleared enough to make recognition easy, the cattlemen began to gather. There were fewer of them than had gone into the fight. Nick saw that Herb Simpson had come up with his men. They took stock. Six cattlemen had paid the supreme price for the peace that finally had been won, while the effort to upset it had cost the other side three times that number.

The Basques moved the sheep farther south at once, taking them to the next water. They would, Pilar said, gradually trail the bands on until they reached the Southern Pacific in Utah, where they would ship. Perhaps Coyle had heirs to the money for his sheep. If not it would be given to charity.

"Will you be back?" Herb Simpson asked before they left.

Pilar smiled at him. "One Corta I think will stay, *señor.*"

"But you and Tomas," Simpson said earnestly. "We want you here. We need you. The Lilyville men who were in this fight and pulled out know they can't stay in this country. They'll have sense enough to leave voluntarily. And if we had somebody like you Cortas up there, we wouldn't ever worry about having sheepers next to us again."

Pilar's brown eyes glistened. "That is from the heart, *señor.* And it is from the heart that I say Pilar and Tomas Corta will return to the high country. No longer is there the hate of the cowmen. It is not the work of men that makes them good or bad. Now we know that."

The dead and wounded were left in the charge of Simpson and his men until vehicles could be sent to transport them. The rest rode home, tired but already feeling the first sweet easing of a reliable peace. The war had been forced upon them. They had won it and felt they had a right to this content.

Nick, Pat, Laramie and Bike rode into Moccasin at dusk. Lily was there with the doctor she had made such a long, desperate ride to bring. Carlita was there, and old Quince.

"He's going to live," Lily said happily. "Pace will pull through."

Quince looked at Nick inquiringly. "How'd it go?"

"The Corta brothers are taking Coyle's sheep to the railroad," Nick said, and heard Carlita's relieved sigh. "They're coming back to the high country, and I've got a little ranch up there I'm going back to now. With the remaining Corta, if she'd like to go."

Carlita's eyes were shining. "She would like to very much," she said.

Center Point Large Print
600 Brooks Road / PO Box 1
Thorndike, ME 04986-0001 USA

(207) 568-3717

US & Canada:
1 800 929-9108
www.centerpointlargeprint.com